LIGHTING CANDLES IN THE DARK

*Prepared by the
Religious Education Committee
of Friends General Conference*

A Revision of *Candles in the Dark*

Editorial Committee:
*Marnie Clark
Elinor Briggs
Carol Passmore*

*A Publication of Friends General Conference
of the Religious Society of Friends (Quakers)*

The Religious Education Committee would like to acknowledge the editorial help of:

Sharon Annis	Mary Lee Hicks
Joan Broadfield	Kay Hollister
Janice Domanik	Ilse Reich
Marty Grundy	Carolyn Terrell
Abby Hadley	Elizabeth Yeats

Special funding was graciously made available by:

Philadelphia Yearly Meeting Publications Committee
The Meeting Fund of Chapel Hill Friends Meeting
The Sarah Bowers Fund of Kennett Friends Meeting

Cover design and art work by Sylvia Thomas
Book design and layout by Sheilah Thomas
Printed by Gilliland Printing, Inc.

The Editorial Committee is especially grateful to these children, who helped us by evaluating stories and giving us their reactions and suggestions:

Isaac Bloom	Lyrica Hammann	Eva Paige
Heather Brutz	Devin Helfrich	Hanna Passmore
Brian Burkhardt	Caitlin Hollister	Emily Richardson
Stephen Domanik	Emily Hollister	Suzanna Roettger
Jessica Eastman	Rebecca Hollister	Sam Schifman
Jesse Foster-Stout	Susannah Hollister	Carolyn Shoemaker
Brook Freeman	Tyson Intile	Zack Sionakides
Heather Freeman	Jesse Kerman	Ethan Smith
Avram Golden-Trist	Allison Kinnucan	Rachel Tyson
Michael Goren	Lindsey Kirk	Leif Wettemann
Neil Gray	Macelle Mahala	Magdelina Zopf
	Michael Morehouse	

CONTENTS

Group III: Acts of Loving Service

Group IV: Fairness and Equality

Group V: Belonging and Care of the Earth

PREFACE

Children work on many tasks as they are growing up. Perhaps the most important is figuring out who they are and what they stand for. This is a lifelong task; answers change and become more clearly delineated with increasing maturity and experience in meeting life's challenges. But the foundation and direction are set in the early years.

In this ongoing task of self-definition, no influences are more important than the examples the child experiences of how other people meet situations of danger, loss, unfairness, and unwanted life changes. If we want our children to value courage, loving service, and fairness for all God's children, we need to expose them to real people acting out these values, however difficult the circumstances and regardless of whether they themselves are rewarded for their actions.

Stories are an ideal extension of first-hand experience. People from many historical places and many cultural settings can come alive as children see them meeting the particular difficulties of their time and place. If these people meet their difficulties with courage and love and service, children are helped to develop the faith that this is the way the Creator designed the world to work. Through stories, children can come to see themselves as God's hands in the world, helping make things safer and better for people and for the planet itself. By meeting many people who believe that life is precious and dare to respond to hate or unfairness with love and nurturing instead of more hate, children can see the power of one individual to make a difference.

This revision of *Candles in the Dark,* like the original edition, has grown out of a wish to help our children learn the ways of peace and align themselves with the "ocean of light" that George Fox saw overcoming the "ocean of darkness." To teach young people to "live a philosophy of love, as opposed to hate," the original editors chose stories that would help children:

- ❖ Feel with Courage, Forgiveness, and Friendliness.
- ❖ Think in terms of Justice and Truth.
- ❖ Act with Self-Control, and in a spirit of Brotherhood and Service.

Each of the stories in *Candles in the Dark* was identified with one of these values.

For this revision, we have kept many of the same stories, while seeking more twentieth-century examples of these values. Also, in our increasingly interdependent and ecology-conscious world, we have sought to counterbalance our society's overemphasis on individualism with stories about social witness for fairness, and about people working for community and for the well-being of the ecosystem of which we are a part.

This new collection retains close to half of the original stories. As before, it spans the centuries and its characters come from many parts of the world and many different societies. Most stories are true or based on actual events. Many are about Quakers. Again the stories are intended especially for children between seven and twelve. We see the stories as a resource for parents and teachers to read or tell to children, as well as stories that the older children will be able to read themselves. In a number of cases, brief "setting" statements have been added to introduce stories that may need some explanation for today's children.

In this new edition, the stories have been grouped under five values:

I: Courage and Nonviolence

II: The Power of Love

III: Acts of Loving Service

IV: Fairness and Equality

V: Belonging and Care of the Earth

Each group ends with a longer story showing a whole life expressing that value. Most of the stories in the last two groups are new to this edition, since these groups focus on values not specifically targeted in the original edition.

The first edition was very successful, was quickly reprinted, and then sold out. Plans for a revision were started when Philadelphia Yearly Meeting, the earlier publisher, gave permission to Friends General Conference to prepare and publish a new edition.

Two successive subcommittees of the Religious Education Committee of Friends General Conference have worked on this revision in the intervening years. The Editorial Committee has worked under the guidance of a project team representing both the Religious Education and Publication Committees of Friends General Conference. Reviewers from both committees have read the stories and offered helpful comments. Our grateful thanks go especially to those named on the copyright page.

Marnie Clark
Elinor Briggs
Carol Passmore

November 1991

"I shall light a candle of understanding in thine heart . . ."

Apocrypha, Old Testament
II Esdras, XIV 25

HE WAS READY TO HIT ME

By Calhoun Geiger

This story begins in 1947. It was a beautiful spring day and I was in Florida, plowing a field for a friend of mine. I had been a conscientious objector during World War II and was very happy to be back at my home farming, as I had done before the war.

A group of convicts was working on a large drain pipe near one end of the field. I stopped close to the dense, scrubby bushes that hedged that side of the field and knelt to adjust and grease the plow. As I was pumping grease into the bearings with a grease-gun, a slight noise caused me to glance up. Out of the bushes came a man. He was wearing the striped black and white uniform of a convict. Over his shoulder he carried a heavy club, the handle of a tool.

He stopped only a few feet from me, and his first words were, "I need money awful bad and whatever you have I'm going to take."

Instantly, I realized that I could neither run away nor fight him. With his club almost over my head, there would be no chance of either. So I did what he least expected. I looked up from my work and directly at him. "If you need help that badly,"

I said, "why don't you just say so, and we won't have any rough stuff about it."

I went back to greasing the plow. He stood there a moment and then lowered his club. When he did this, I said to him, "So, you're running away. Do you realize you will be a hunted man?"

He said he did, but the bosses on the chain gang were mean. We talked a few more minutes, while I continued to grease and adjust the plow. Suddenly, he dropped the club to the ground.

"You win," he said. "I'm going back." He turned and without another word disappeared into the bushes.

After muttering a prayer of thanks for the strength and guidance I had felt, I cranked up the tractor and continued with my work. Whenever I was near the side of the field where the convicts were still working, I tried to see if my man was with them, but it was too far to be sure. I supposed that this was the end of my contact with him. It is hard to believe how mistaken I was.

The next part of this story comes several years later. I had quit farming and become Director of the Boys' Clubs in my home town of Jacksonville, Florida. One evening, I had been at a meeting and was anxious to get home. Unfortunately, just before I reached an intersection, two cars hit each other head-on. As I approached, I saw the two drivers, apparently unhurt, get out of their cars and run at each other, fists flying. Almost at once one of the men went down, and the other, who seemed to be furious, began to kick the fallen man and to strike him with a wrench he held.

I was sorely tempted to turn the corner toward home, but quite clearly came the words, "No, Calhoun! You must stop and help!" So, a bit unwillingly, I thought about what I could do. There was no time to hunt a phone and call the police. It looked to me as if a man might be dead almost at once unless the kicking and beating could be stopped.

Again the little inward voice spoke. "You are strong and those muscles were not given to you only for sport. Move quickly!"

I jumped out of my car and crossed the short space between me and the two men: one unconscious on the pavement, the other still intent on his enraged attack. I moved behind him with only the dim light from a nearby service station to show me the way. Before he knew what was happening, I wrapped my arms around him, clamping his arms to his sides. He struggled, but I just held on. We tripped on a broken place in the pavement and fell with a crash near where the other man lay unconscious. I still just held on. I did not strike or otherwise hurt him. Soon a man appeared from the service station and offered help. I asked him to call the police.

The police arrived quickly. I was still holding the struggling man, who was calling me various unflattering names. The other man still lay unconscious nearby. The police brought plenty of handcuffs and were about to cuff me also until I explained what had happened. They became very appreciative and soon let me go home to my wife, who was wondering why I was so late. After I left, I realized and regretted that I had not looked at the faces of either of the men on that dark night.

The story doesn't end here either. Several years later I was volunteering time helping with recreation programs in a local mental hospital. One day a worker at the hospital called me to say that a former patient had called her. His name, he said, was George Harris. He had recognized me at the hospital. I said I didn't know any George Harris, but the hospital worker said he had told her he was the escaped prisoner who had threatened me out in the field. He was also the car driver who knocked the other man down and, he said, would have killed him if I had not come out of the darkness and stopped him. If not for me, he'd be a murderer.

After that, he'd had a mental breakdown and been in a mental hospital for a while. When he got out, he went to work and started saving his money. Now he wanted to mail her a gift to give me. She tried to persuade him to bring it to me himself, but he wouldn't. So a few days later I stopped by her office. When we opened the package from George Harris, there was a

Bulova self-winding watch, which still runs well even as I tell this story, twenty some years later.

I thought *this* was the end of the story, but it wasn't. Although my family moved several times, George Harris kept track of me. He would write to let me know that he was doing well, and he sent me gifts several times—a beautiful woodworker's workbench, a pair of leather boots just my size, and a Hamilton "Railway Special" watch. I always wrote to thank him at a General Delivery address on the parcels.

He never answered my letters, but one day, as I was building a chimney at Carolina Friends School in North Carolina, a car with Virginia license plates pulled into the drive. The driver walked up to me and said, "Cal Geiger, I believe."

"Yes," I said, "and who may you be?"

"I'm George Harris," he said.

He told me then that he had gone to school and become a teacher. He had a wife and two children. He said his health was poor now, and he wanted to see me and thank me in person before he died. Then he walked to his car and left.

I know that what one says and does can make a big difference. I made a difference to George Harris, but I also made a difference for myself. When I think of the whole story and what it has meant for me, I have an overwhelming feeling of being very grateful for having known George Harris.

FEATHER OF PEACE

By the Committee

Setting: The time was 1777, just a year after the Declaration of Independence had been signed. The thirteen American colonies were fighting to win their freedom from powerful England.

For the settlers in Saratoga County, in the valley of the Hudson River north of Albany, it was a scary time. Both armies were camped not far away, and both of them were sending scouting parties through the valley nearly every day. Scouting parties were small groups of soldiers and guides. Besides trying to find out what the other army was up to, each scouting party was looking for food for the armies. They just took whatever they could find, including grain, cows, sheep, and pigs.

Most scary for the settlers was the fact that Indians were often used in the scouting parties because they knew the countryside so well. Most of the area was not settled yet and was pretty wild. The Indians were angry at the settlers for spoiling their hunting and for pushing them back from land they had always used. There were many stories of their torturing and killing settlers—and sometimes scalping them. And they spoke a different language so it was hard to talk to them.

It got so dangerous for the settlers that the American government finally said it could not protect them and they should all leave and go back east where it was safer. In July that year, a whole family in that valley, the Allens, had been killed at their dinner table.

Most families did leave, but several Quaker families decided to stay. They had always gotten along well with the Indians, and they hated to leave their new farms. They had built a log meetinghouse just the year before, at what would later be called Easton.

So they watched all their neighbors load up what they could carry. Some had wagons, some went on horseback. Some used sledges, dragged along the ground. Many more just fled on foot. Most of their possessions had to be left behind.

By September, only the Quaker families were left—the families of Zebulon Hoxsie and his brother-in-law, Rufus Hall, who had started their meeting four years before, and a few other families who had come to join them. The nearest Quaker meeting was another new meeting nearly fifty miles away, at East Hoosack, Massachusetts.

In the East Hoosack meeting was a young man named Robert Nisbet, who had come to America from Scotland eleven years before. After some time in Boston and Nova Scotia, he had come to East Hoosack, where he became a Friend and later, a traveling minister. He was outspoken against slavery and consistently refused to wear anything made by slaves. He could speak both English and French.

One morning that September, Robert Nisbet woke up at 4 AM and felt a strong urge to visit the Easton Meeting for their midweek worship. It meant walking through the wilderness alone for two whole days, but he started right out, and he got there in time. He sat next to Zebulon Hoxsie on the facing bench, and the meeting settled into silence.

After a long, deep silence, Robert Nisbet stood up and gave a strange message. He said, "You did well, Friends, to stay on valiantly in your homes when all your neighbors have fled. The report of your courage and faith has reached us in East

Hoosack, and God has charged me to come on foot through the wilderness all these miles to meet with you today, and to bear to you these two messages:

The Beloved of God shall dwell in safety.
and He shall cover you with his feathers all the day long.

You shall not be afraid for the terror by night nor for
the arrow that flieth by day."

While the grown-ups were pondering these strange words, a little boy in the front row saw a head appear at a window, then another, and another. They were Indians! The boy raised his arm to point at them, but his mother put down his arm, continuing her silent worship.

By this time, other worshipers had become aware of the visitors, but the silent worship continued. Robert Nisbet looked up and saw them and felt called to go out to talk to them. He rose quietly and walked down the aisle and out the open door.

Outside, he found a small group of Indians with a frightened young prisoner. The Indians were in full war paint and carried weapons. One had a dried-up scalp hanging from his belt.

"Any weapons inside?" asked the leader in French.

"No, no weapons," answered Robert Nisbet promptly, speaking in French also. "We are worshiping the Great Spirit. Will you join us?"

Wary and suspicious, the leader moved to the door to see for himself and took a few steps inside. For what seemed like hours, he stood there, straight and still as a statue, his piercing eyes looking carefully at each man. But of course, the Friends were totally unarmed—no guns, no swords, no knives.

During this time, most heads remained bowed in worship, but Zebulon Hoxsie, on the facing bench, was smiling a loving welcome. Finally, satisfied that there were no weapons, the Indian leader gave Zebulon Hoxsie a long, angry, scowling look, then slowly dropped his eyes. Love had won. Motioning to the others to follow him, he put his weapons against the wall, walked quietly to the center of the room and sat down on the floor. The others did likewise.

The silence continued and deepened as the sunlight streamed through the open windows and Indians and Friends worshiped together in the little log room.

When the hour ended, Zebulon Hoxsie walked to the Indian leader and shook hands warmly with him. Though he could not speak French, he had no trouble using signs to invite the visitors to his home. An earlier raiding party had taken most of his supplies, but he had been able to hide a round of cheese, and his wife had baked bread the day before. So he placed bread and cheese on the table and motioned to his guests to eat. They did so with obvious pleasure and thanked him with nods and smiles. The records say that they let their prisoner eat too, but do not make it clear whether they released him.

When they had finished, the leader said in broken English that they had come to kill. But when they found people worshiping the Great Spirit, with no guns or knives, the Great Spirit had told him not to kill these people.

Then he took out a white feather. Solemnly, he walked back to the meetinghouse and fastened the feather above the door.

"Safe, all," he said, with a wide sweep of his hand to include all those present. "Indians and you—friends."

And then the little band took their leave and were soon lost to sight in the forest.

Today, a white frame meetinghouse stands near where the little log one stood in 1777. The gravestones in the little cemetery under the trees show that Friends have been worshiping in Easton Meeting for more than 200 years since that bright September day. And there is still a white feather above the door.

Note: The Committee found several quite different versions of this story and visited Easton Meeting to talk with several current members. Some of the details will never be known for sure. Our version represents our best judgment of what may have happened. In writing it, we have drawn on material in: "Washington County NY Quaker Records" in *NY Genealogical and Biographical Records*, 1915, vol 46, pp 122-125, "Fierce Feathers" by L. Violet Hodgkins in *A Book of Quaker Saints*, 1917; *The Feather of Peace*, written and originally published by Walter and Mildred Kalhoe; *The Story of Fierce Feathers*, by Elizabeth M. Lantz, with help from Anna Curtis (1961); "Feathers of Peace" by Dorothy Williams in *Quaker History*, vol 65, Spring 1976, #1, pp 32-34; the script of a play used at Easton Meeting; and personal communications.

THE BOOT UNDER THE BED

By Murry P. Engle and the Committee

The old stone inn was warm inside and welcoming to Elizabeth Fry. But in spite of her heavy wool shawl and long wool skirt, she was chilled through and through. She had just returned from a day spent like many days before, working in the cold and drafty women's side of the prison at Bristol.

"Those filthy stone rooms, with the cold and dripping walls!" she was thinking as she passed the big cheerful fire that warmed the main room of the inn. "They are no fit place for anyone to stay in, no matter what crimes they have committed! And those poor little children shut up, too! How I'd like to take them out into the sunshine and let them run! All that yelling and fighting! I need to find something to occupy their minds and their hands." So ran her thoughts as she climbed the winding stairs to her room.

As soon as she opened the door, she sensed something strange about the room. The small-paned windows were still closed, as she had left them in the morning, but a dresser drawer was partly open, with a shawl dangling from it. Glancing

Based on material in *Victories Without Violence*, compiled by A. Ruth Fry, originally published by Peace Book Club, England, 1939, republished in 1986 by Ocean Tree Books, Santa Fe, NM.

down at the floor, she saw the candle from the night stand lying broken on the bare boards. Then she gave a little gasp. There, under the bed, just visible below the patchwork quilt, was the sole of a man's boot.

What should she do? To give herself time to think, she went quietly to the dresser and closed the drawer. Then she picked up the broken candle. Now she had reached a decision.

She knelt down beside the boot. She could hear someone breathing hard under the bed, perhaps terrified at the prospect of being caught. "Dear Lord," she began, "please forgive this man for what he has done. May thy goodness enter his heart and help him to improve his ways." Her voice was soft and kind.

The boot stirred.

"Dear Lord, this man is confused and needs thy guidance so that he will steal no more."

The man crawled out from under the bed. He was very thin, with a dark, stubbly beard and long, uncombed hair. "Why are you praying for me?" he asked gruffly. "Why don't you call the innkeeper and get it over with?

"The Lord is the only one I'll call on," said Elizabeth as she rose from her knees. She was still a little bit afraid, but she looked at him kindly. "Thee must have had a very special reason for coming to my room."

His shoulders drooped.

"Can't thee tell me what it was?" she continued. The man remained silent, and Elizabeth waited.

"I'm hungry, Ma'am," he said at last. "I've been hungry for days. I've been stealing scraps of food, but they didn't fill the empty hole here in my stomach. I needed money—for real food. I was looking for a warm coat too.

"I'm glad thee came to my room," said Elizabeth. "I think I can help thee."

The man looked at her in utter amazement. He had never been treated so kindly before, not even that time when he was working as a footman on a stagecoach.

Elizabeth pulled a heavy sweater from the drawer. "This is my husband's sweater," she said. "I think it will fit thee. Now let's go downstairs and have dinner."

The man's pale face broke into a broad grin. "You're sure good to me," he said. "You could have had me put in prison—or will you anyway?" His eyes suddenly darted wildly toward the window.

"No," said Elizabeth. "I know too much about prisons to send anyone there." And seeing his puzzlement, she added, "I'll tell thee about it while we eat."

Elizabeth led the man downstairs to the big hall of the inn. While he consumed a big plate of boiled mutton and potatoes, she told him about her work in the women's prisons. Then he gave her a full account of his own troubles.

He had been in prison three times—the first time for owing money he couldn't pay, the second time for stealing, and the third time just because of his reputation. Since the last time, he had not been able to get a job. His clothes were worn and dirty and he looked so bad that no one trusted him enough to give him work. He was determined never to be thrown in jail again, so he had almost starved to death before coming at last to Elizabeth's room.

Elizabeth was moved by his story. It was like so many of the sad stories she had heard from the women in the prison.

In her practical way, she thought first about the man's need for a job. She talked with him about what work he might do and where he might look for it. When they parted, she gave him some money for soap and a clean set of clothes.

The man left with strength in his body and hope in his heart. Elizabeth returned to her room with a deep sense of peace, grateful that she had been led to respond to him with love rather than with fear.

THOMAS LURTING
AND THE PIRATES

By the Committee

Setting: This is a true story of a man who changed from an enthusiastic fighter to a Quaker who refused to hurt anyone—even when bloodthirsty pirates captured his ship.

Thomas Lurting was born in England, probably about the same time as George Fox. But they never met. In fact, Thomas was kidnapped by a "press gang" when he was fourteen and forced to serve in the British navy. Actually, he didn't mind too much. He was eager to serve his king and his country, and he wanted to win honor and glory in the war against Spain.

Thomas became known as a fearless fighter and in time became first mate on a battleship. He had 200 men under his command, and one of his jobs was to see that they attended the Chaplain's Sunday services.

All went well until some young Quakers joined the crew. They were brave and strong, good workers and good fighters who had not yet heard about the Quaker peace testimony. But they would not take off their hats to show honor to the captain

Based on "The Gay Story of Thomas and the Pirates" in *Quakers Courageous* by Frances Margaret Fox, New York: Lothrop, Lee and Shepard, 1941.

because they believed that all people were equal in God's sight, and they refused to take part in the Sunday services that everyone on shipboard was supposed to attend. Thomas was ordered to whip them, a common punishment in those days.

He tried to reason with them. Was it really worth a beating? If they would admit they were wrong, he would put the whip away. But they wouldn't, so he did beat them—then and many more times, but with increasing feelings of discomfort and sympathy for them. And he listened when one of the youngest— still in his teens—explained about his belief that all people have God's light inside them. Thomas began to pray, "Please, God, don't let me become a Quaker. I'd rather die!"

Finally, one day, he told the captain he could not beat the Quakers any more. The captain tried to find other men to do it, but one look at Thomas and they refused too. The captain was furious. He read to Thomas parts of the Bible that he thought proved the Quakers were wrong. Thomas wanted to believe him, but he just couldn't.

Not long after that an epidemic broke out. One man after another fell ill with a dreadful disease. The Quakers, ignoring their own fevers and weakness, gently cared for their ill ship-mates and helped them get well.

And in the battle that followed, they fought well, indifferent to their own safety. But they would take no booty. When one ship defeated another in battle, the captain usually divided the money, gold, and jewels from the captured vessel and gave some to his crew. The Quakers felt that this was stealing, and they wanted no part of it. That was just fine with the captain and other crew members: it meant more loot for them. By this time, Thomas had become a Quaker too.

Then one day, in the midst of a ferocious battle, young Thomas Lurting had what Quakers call an *opening*. As he got the cannon ready to fire, he suddenly thought, "What if I killed a man!" He decided that killing was wrong, even when someone was ordering him to do it. After the battle, he told the captain that he would not fight any more. The other Quakers said they would not fight any more either.

Again the captain was furious. He drew his sword. Thomas, without hesitation, stepped forward, prepared to die.

The captain was stunned. He didn't want to murder anyone—especially his own brave boatswain's mate. He sheathed his sword and turned away. But at the first opportunity, he put Thomas and the other Quakers ashore.

After that, press gangs kidnapped Thomas again several times. He was a big, powerful man who looked as if he would be a good sailor and a strong fighter. But each time he was put on a ship, he said he would not fight. Several captains argued with him, beat him, threatened him, and tried to starve him, but eventually gave up and let him go.

Finally, England's war with Spain was over, and Thomas got a job on a merchant ship with a Quaker captain. He thought his troubles were over. Little did he know what was ahead!

They had not been at sea long when Turkish pirates stopped them. The pirates took control of the ship and put some of their men on it to force the English crew to sail it toward Algiers, a port friendly to the Turks. The English sailors knew that in Algiers they would be put in prison or sold as slaves.

Thomas told the crew that the Lord had spoken to him, assuring him that the ship would not get to Algiers. But, said Thomas, the Lord was firm that they should obey the Turks.

The crew trusted Thomas. So all the men cooperated with their Turkish captors. The English crew followed their orders cheerfully and with courtesy. The pirate captain and the Quaker captain shared the same cabin. The Turkish crew began to relax and even started sleeping in separate cabins.

A little later, Thomas said he had a plan for overcoming the Turks so they could head back to England. The sailors were overjoyed.

"I'll kill one or two!" said one.

"And I'll cut as many throats as you will have me!" said another.

Thomas said sternly, "If I thought you would touch a Turk to kill him, I would tell the Turks myself!" He had a different plan and promised the captain that there would be no bloodshed. The sailors promised to do as he said.

By this time, the pirate ship had sailed out of sight, and the English ship was alone on the wide ocean. One night, while the Turks were asleep, the English crew crept into the pirates' cabins, took all their weapons, and locked the doors. Then they turned the ship back toward England.

On their way, they stopped at Majorca, a Spanish port. Like most of the Christian world, the Spanish hated the Turks. The captain knew that if their Turkish prisoners were found, they would be seized and sold into slavery—if they were not put to death at once. So the pirates were kept hidden on the ship.

But when a friend of his visited him on shipboard, the captain could not resist telling his amazing story. As he left the ship, the friend offered to buy some of the Turks himself. The captain indignantly refused. But soon after, word reached the captain that Spanish officials were on the way to the ship—accompanied by his friend. He knew they would search the ship and seize the Turks.

In order to leave the port as quickly as possible, he called the pirates up on deck to help his men with the sails. Again, the pirates swarmed the ship's decks, this time following the orders of the Quaker captain, who was trying to save their lives.

Back at sea, the ship continued its course toward England. But when the Turks found out where they were headed, they were terrified. It became clear that life for Turks in England would be as painful—and perhaps as brief—as life for the English in Algiers.

One evening, when only the captain and Thomas and the helmsman were on deck, the pirates began to threaten the captain, who was a small man. Thomas realized they were about to throw the captain into the sea. All the other sailors, like the pirates earlier, were asleep below.

Quick as a flash, Thomas stamped his foot on the deck, his heavy boot booming against the planks, waking the sleeping men below. Realizing something was wrong, they ran up onto the deck and surrounded the Turks. Angry and desperate, the Turks were ready to fight them all.

Thomas had hidden all the weapons, so his men had grabbed shovels, crowbars, and other tools on their way up, but Thomas made them put down everything they had. Then he turned to the pirate captain and told him to go below. Quietly, the man obeyed. The other pirates did the same. Their mutiny was over.

But the incident worried Thomas. He did not want to take the Turks to England. He told the captain of his concern, and the two men agreed that the Turks should be able to go back to their homes. So again the ship turned around and headed the other way—toward Algiers.

But returning enemy sailors to an enemy country was no easy matter. When the English ship neared the Algerian coast, it would be in enemy waters, risking capture itself. If it were sighted, they would be helpless.

So when they got a few miles from their destination and could see the shore, Thomas and the captain anchored their vessel. They would put the Turks into a row boat for the last, most dangerous part of the journey.

Three trembling volunteers said they would row the pirates to shore with Thomas. They begged to tie up the pirates, but Thomas would not let them. Instead, he had five of the pirates sit in the laps of the other five.

It must have been a funny sight—five pirates in the laps of five other pirates, in a small boat rowed by four Englishmen— but no one laughed. The pirates sat very still, knowing they were almost free; the English scanned the shore carefully as they came closer, looking for signs of Turks in the bushes. Once a sailor shouted that he saw some, and the pirates jumped up, nearly upsetting the boat. But it was a false alarm, and Thomas made them sit down again.

Finally the boat got to where the water was shallow enough for the Turks to wade ashore. One by one, they climbed out of the boat. The Englishmen handed them some bread and their weapons, and then the pirates sloshed away toward the land.

"We parted in great love," Thomas reported to the captain later. "We stayed in sight of land till they had gone up the hill. They shook their caps at us, and we ours at them."

Back to England sailed the ship, then. But that's not the end of the story.

When they got to England, they found a crowd on the dock to greet them, including even the king of England—Charles II—and his brother, the Duke of York. Somehow, news of their adventure had reached home before they did.

While all the others doffed their hats and bowed low before the king, the captain and Thomas kept their hats on and their backs straight as their monarch greeted them.

The king did not look entirely pleased. He made the captain tell him the whole story and listened intently to every word. At the end, he scolded the captain: "You have done like a fool, for you might have had good gain from them."

Then he turned to Thomas and said, "You should have brought the Turks to me!"

Thomas looked at his king. "I thought it was better for them to be in their own country," he replied.

And then the king showed what kind of ruler he really was. He looked at these two subjects, who had brought neither booty nor slaves, and who would not even bow or take off their caps to show their respect for him. Instead of being angry, he thought it was funny. He threw back his head and laughed.

THE MISSIONARY'S WIFE

By Pearl S. Buck

Setting: This is a true story about a family who went to China many years ago. They went to tell people about Jesus. At first, the people listened to them eagerly, but this changed when the usual rains did not come. People began to think their gods were punishing them for listening to the foreigners.

D ay after day through the Spring no rain fell, and the farmers, waiting for the floods of the rainy season to fill their rice fields, saw their young crops dry up before their eyes.

Carie, the missionary's wife, ever sensitive to changes in the moods of people, felt such a change in the temper of the people in the city. Few came to the little chapel where her husband, Andrew, preached. One Sunday there was not a single person.

The next day Wang Amah, the faithful Chinese servant, came back from her marketing and said to Carie, "It is better for us not to go out now on the street. The people say the gods are angry because foreigners have come into the city. There has never been a drought like this before, and this is the first year there have been foreigners in the city to live."

One hot August afternoon when Andrew was away from home, Carie sat by the window sewing. She heard a whisper of voices beneath the open window. Two men were plotting something.

"Tonight at midnight," they said, "tonight at midnight we will force the gates and kill them. Then rain will come."

Carie rose quickly and went to find Wang Amah. "Go out and listen about the streets," she said. "Find out if you can what is being planned for this night." And then she whispered what she had heard.

Without a word, Wang Amah put on her poorest coat and went out. In a little while she came back, her eyes staring. She shut all the doors carefully and then went near to Carie and put her lips to Carie's ear.

"Oh, my mistress," she panted, "they are coming to kill you tonight—you and the children. Every white person is to be killed."

Carie stood still, saying nothing. Then she went toward Wang Amah and taking the hard, faithful brown hands in her own said, "I am not afraid. I will go and pray to my God."

Carie went to her room, shut the door and fell upon her knees by the bed. She prayed, "If it is Thy will, save us, but in any case, help me not to be afraid." She knelt for a long time then, thinking of what she must do. For a long time she was silent, waiting. At last she rose, somewhat amazed at her own calmness. She would trust in God, silent as He was, and not fear what men could do to her.

That night she put the children to bed early and then sat quietly sewing. Gradually it came to her what she must do. The murmur of the city drummed through the stifling, dusty air. She listened to it, striving tensely to catch a change in its tempo. About midnight the change came. The murmur rose and seemed to eddy about the walls of the house. The hour was coming. Carie rose and called softly to Wang Amah, who sat silent in the shadow of the court, "Wang Amah, please prepare the tea now."

Then she went downstairs and set out cups and plates upon the oval table and placed cakes on plates. Then when all was ready as though for a feast she swept and made the room spotlessly neat and set the chairs as for guests. Then she went to the court and to the front gate and threw it wide open.

On the threshold stood a vanguard of men, their faces invisible in the darkness of the hot night. They drew back into the blackness but she did not seem to see them, nor did she falter. She went back to the house and left the door open into the court, turned the oil lamp high, so that the light streamed outside, and then went upstairs and roused the three children and dressed them and brought them downstairs. They were astonished and silent with the strangeness of the proceeding, but she talked to them naturally, sang a little song to them, and set them on the matting of the floor and gave them their Sunday toys to play with and they fell to playing happily. Then she took up her sewing again and sat down. Wang Amah had brought in pots of tea, and she stood behind the children, motionless, her face expressionless.

All about the house the murmur increased until it was a roar of many voices. When the voices became articulate and very near, Carie rose casually and went to the door and called out, "Will you come in, please?"

They were already in the court then and at the sound of her voice they swelled forward, a mass of sullen, angry men . . . , in their hands sticks and clubs and knives. She called again kindly, her voice made bright by sheer will, "Come in, friends, neighbors! I have tea prepared."

The men paused at this uncertainly. A few pressed forward. Carie poured the tea busily and came forward bearing a cup in both her hands as the polite custom was. She presented it to the tall, surly, half-naked man who seemed to be the leader. His mouth gaped in amazement but he took the cup helplessly. Carie smiled her most brilliant smile upon the faces that gleamed in the light from the wide-flung door.

"Will you come in and drink tea for yourselves?" she said. "And sit down also. I am sorry my humble house has not enough seats, but you are welcome to what I have."

Then she stepped back to the table and pretended to busy herself there. The children stopped playing and Edwin ran to her side. But she reassured them gently, "Nothing to be afraid of, darlings. Just some people come to see what we look like. They haven't seen Americans before."

The crowd began to edge into the room, staring, gaping, momentarily diverted. Someone whispered, "Strange, she is not afraid!"

"Why should I fear my neighbors?" she asked in surprise.

Others began to examine the furniture, the curtains, the organ. One touched a note and Carie showed him how to make the sound come. Then she slipped into the seat and began to play softly and to sing, in Chinese, "Jesus, Thy Name I Love."

Dead silence filled the room until she finished. At last the men looked at each other hesi-tatingly. One muttered, "There is nothing here— only this woman and these child-ren—"

"I go home," said another sim-ply and went out.

Others, still sullen, lingered, and the leader halted to look at the children. He held out his hand to Arthur and the rosy, friendly lit-tle boy, having seen brown faces about him all his life, smiled and seized the man's lean dark forefinger. The man laughed delightedly and cried out, "Here is a good one to play!"

The crowd gathered about the children then, watched them, began to grow voluble in their comments, picked up the American toys to examine and play with them. Carie, watching, was in an agony of fear lest a rough movement might frighten one of the children and so change the temper of the men. At last the leader rose and announced loudly, "There is nothing more to do here. I go home."

It was the signal to follow. One by one, with backward stares, they passed into the court and into the street. Carie sat down again, suddenly faint, and taking the baby into her lap rocked him gently. The men, lingering at the threshold of the gate, looked last upon her thus.

When they were all gone Carie lifted Edith in her arms and taking Edwin by the hand she led the way upstairs. She bathed the children again in cool water and put them back to bed. Then she went down and closed the gate of the court upon the street, now silent and empty. At the door of the house she paused. A wind had risen out of the southeast—fresh and cool with the coolness of the distant sea.

She went upstairs to bed then and lay still, listening. Would the wind bring rain? She lay sleepless for a long hour and fell at last into a light sleep, and later awoke. Upon the tile roof above her was the music of rain pouring down, streaming from the corners of the house, splashing upon the stones of the court. . . .

THE KEEPER OF THE KEYS

By Alfred Hassler

Setting: In the 1940s, before World War II had come to Asia, Japanese armies were sweeping down through China, taking control wherever they went. It was a time of terror for those whose villages were captured, and also for any foreign teachers and missionaries who were still there.

A few miles outside a little Chinese village stood an American university. It was abandoned, for its teachers and students had fled as the Japanese troops approached. Only one man had stayed on, an American missionary named Merlin Bishop. He could hear the rattle of machine guns in the distance, and the frightening sound was coming closer each day.

One day, Japanese soldiers came along the road. Merlin saw that they were a dirty, tired-looking bunch. It was a small group, a sort of advance guard. They would trot along the road a hundred yards and then squat down, set up a machine gun, and spray the road ahead with bullets. Merlin was standing at the gate as they went by, but they paid no attention to him.

By the next day, the nearby village had become a field headquarters for the army, and Merlin's troubles began. As he

Adapted by the Committee from *Courage in Both Hands* by Allan A. Hunter. Copyright© 1962 by Allan A. Hunter. Reprinted by permission of Ballantine Books, a Division of Random House Inc.

had expected, the officers noticed the nice University buildings and wanted to use them. Soon a group called on him and demanded the keys.

Merlin refused, politely but firmly. He explained that the property belonged to churches in America. It was their college, and he was not free to hand it over to anyone else. They talked about it for an hour and a half, with Merlin remaining courteous and friendly but firm. Finally the Japanese were convinced and left.

Unfortunately, that was not the end. About every two weeks, the troops in the village changed, and each new group had to be persuaded all over again. Through it all, Merlin did his best to remain calm and friendly.

Then came a major crisis. This time, something had happened to make the officers less patient, less willing to listen to his arguments. Merlin sensed the tension in the air. He knew perfectly well that he was alone and the soldiers could do with him as they pleased. A dead missionary could easily be explained by a stray bullet.

Nevertheless, he greeted them in a friendly way, as always, and refused their request for the keys of the buildings with his usual regretful firmness. This time, though, the soldiers kept getting more angry.

Finally the officer in command said, "Surrender the keys or we shoot you!"

The missionary stood a little straighter. "I have told you how it is," he replied quietly. "I wish you no harm, but I cannot do what you ask. I cannot."

Grimly, the officer counted off three men and lined them up facing the missionary.

"Ready!" he commanded, and rifles were raised to shoulders. He turned to the missionary. "Surrender the keys!"

"I cannot. I have no hatred against you, only the friendliest feelings for you, but I have no right to give away what does not belong to me. I cannot give you the keys."

Merlin thought he saw admiration and baffled wonderment in their eyes, as though they could not understand what could make him stand straight and smiling in the very face of death.

"Aim!" The officer's voice was gruff. "Your last chance," he said. "Surrender the keys!"

There was a pause. Merlin looked directly at the men who stood with leveled rifles facing him. He spoke to them, as one man to other men, as brother to brother.

"I cannot," he said. "You know that I cannot."

The stillness was absolute. The missionary looked steadily at the three men. The officer seemed uncertain, the men uneasy. Then, one at a time, they relaxed. Rifles lowered, embarrassed grins replaced their looks of grim determination.

But the danger had not passed. One man of the firing squad apparently was disgusted and embarrassed at this outcome. He gripped his rifle and glared.

"O God!" Merlin prayed silently, "a little more love. Let me show a little more love."

The soldier had decided. Abruptly, with a bayonet on the end of his rifle, he launched himself full tilt at the missionary.

At the last instant, when the point of his bayonet was not a foot away, Merlin dodged. As the force of the charge carried the man closer, Merlin reached around him and grabbed the rifle. With his other arm, he grasped the man around the shoulders and pulled the man tight against himself. When their eyes met, the man's face was full of fury.

Their glances locked and held for seconds that seemed ages long. Then Merlin smiled at him, and it was like a spring thaw melting the ice on a frozen river. The hatred vanished, and after a long moment, the man smiled back!

That was the end. A few minutes later the soldiers were trailing the missionary into his living quarters—to have tea before their journey back to the village.

NO ONE WOULD EVER KNOW

By Ellen R. Braaf

Emily's heart pounded as Miss Rossiter handed back the graded spelling tests. She slouched in her chair as the paper was put face down on her desk. It would take a while to work up the courage to look at it.

It was possible to get less than zero on those tests. Since Miss Rossiter dictated not just the new spelling words but whole sentences, it was possible to lose points for any word misspelled or for any mistake in punctuation or capitalization. Miss Rossiter said this kind of test keeps students on their toes.

On the other hand, Emily thought as she fingered her test paper, it was possible to get above 100 because Miss Rossiter believed in bonuses. "Ovoviviporous" was the bonus word the week they studied sharks. "Usurpations" was the bonus word the week they studied the Declaration of Independence. Miss Rossiter could afford to be generous with bonus points: No one ever earned them!

Emily looked down at her paper. She rolled up the corner of the test and took a peek. . . . Amazing!

Emily rushed home after school. She charged up the front porch steps two at a time. The screen door banged shut behind her. She chose a magnet that looked like a piece of broccoli and clicked her test to the refrigerator door. "I did it!" she told her mother. "I finally got 100 on a spelling test from Miss Rossiter!" Mom smiled and hugged Emily.

Emily was alone in the kitchen when Janice knocked and came in. Janice was a seventh-grader who excelled in locking herself out of her house next door. She strolled over to the refrigerator and looked at the test. "Mmmmm. . . Emily, how do you spell 'lettuce'."

"Easy," said Emily. "L-E-T-T-U-C-E."

"That's not what you wrote here," said Janice. "Take a look."

Emily looked. Janice was right. In sentence #2, Emily had spelled "lettuce" L-U-T-T-U-C-E.

Emily ripped the test off the refrigerator. The broccoli magnet flew across the room and landed in the dog's water bowl.

"Nice shot," laughed Janice.

"It's not funny!" yelled Emily.

"Why is it such a big deal?" shrugged Janice. "Your teacher thinks you got 100. Your mother does too. No one will ever know."

Emily watched Janice leave the house. Then she ran to her bedroom and dropped onto her bed. "I'll know!" she cried into her pillow. "I'll know!"

Later Emily wandered into the kitchen and threw some cold water on her face from the sink faucet. Her mother was preparing dinner. Emily explained about the misspelled word Janice had found. Her mother was silent. She and Emily stood side by side, peeling carrots.

"I don't see how I could make such a stupid mistake," Emily finally said. "I know how to spell 'lettuce.' Putting a *u* instead of an *e* was *dumb*. But Miss Rossiter didn't catch it. She didn't mark it wrong. That's her mistake."

Mom continued to peel carrots as Emily spoke again. "Janice is a snoop!" she said. "It's none of her business! I wish she didn't live next door.!"

"I think you wish you didn't have such a difficult decision to make," said her mother.

"Yeah," said Emily with a little more calm in her voice. "Mom, what am I going to do?"

Emily's mother brushed a stray hair from her daughter's cheek and gently placed a kiss on her forehead. "This is a tough one, Sweetheart," was all she said.

The next day at school Emily couldn't concentrate. She had a queasy feeling in her stomach. Miss Rossiter graded English essays while the class did math practice problems. When Emily finished her problems, she pushed her book aside, grabbed her spelling test, and went up to Miss Rossiter's desk.

"Excuse me, Miss Rossiter, may I please show you my spelling test?" she asked.

Miss Rossiter looked puzzled. "You did well on this test, Emily," she said as she scanned the paper. "This is your first 100, isn't it?"

Emily nodded. Miss Rossiter turned her attention back to the essays she was grading, and Emily returned to her seat.

"Well, I tried," she told herself. "I gave her a chance to find her mistake and she didn't. I guess that means I get to keep the 100."

But Emily couldn't work. She stared at the teacher. Miss Rossiter's glasses slid down her nose, and when she looked up to adjust them, her eyes met Emily's. Emily reached into her desk, pulled out the test paper, and approached Miss Rossiter again.

"Would you check #2 again?" Emily asked.

Miss Rossiter wrinkled her forehead as she reached for the paper. Emily waited.

"Oh my goodness, Emily," exclaimed Miss Rossiter. "How do you spell 'lettuce'?"

Emily sighed. "L-E-T-T-U-C-E," she said. "I don't know why I wrote a *u* instead of an *e*."

Miss Rossiter picked up her red pen. Emily looked away so she would not see her precious 100 being crossed out. But when she looked back at the paper, she couldn't believe her eyes. Miss Rossiter had written 110. "Congratulations, Emily," she whispered.

"But Miss Rossiter, shouldn't this be a 95?" asked Emily.

"No, it shouldn't," said Miss Rossiter. "I took off five points for the misspelled word, but I gave you fifteen bonus points for your honesty. You earned them the hard way. And I believe you learned a lot more than how to spell 'lettuce'."

At home that afternoon Emily chose a magnet that looked like an apple slice and clicked her spelling test to the refrigerator.

Her mom was proud of her. "Let's celebrate with your favorite dinner, Emily," she said, "pizza and lettuce and tomato salad and. . . ."

"Hold it, Mom!" shouted Emily. "I don't ever want to hear the word 'L-E-T-T-U-C-E' again!"

"OK," laughed her mom. "How about a nice S-P-I-N-A-C-H salad?"

Emily giggled.

HOW CAN I HELP?

By Ram Dass and Paul Gorman

Setting: Ram Dass was a young man from the United States visiting Japan when this happened. He had been taking training in the Japanese martial art of Aikido and he was pretty proud of his skill—and anxious to show it off.

The train clanked and rattled through the suburbs of Tokyo on a drowsy spring afternoon. Our car was comparatively empty—a few housewives with their kids in tow, some old folks going shopping. I gazed absently at the drab houses and dusty hedgerows.

At one station the doors opened, and suddenly the afternoon quiet was shattered by a man bellowing violent, incomprehensible curses. The man staggered into our car. He wore laborer's[1] clothing, and he was big, drunk and dirty. Screaming, he swung at a woman holding a baby. The blow sent her spinning into the laps of an elderly couple. It was a miracle that the baby was unharmed.

Terrified, the couple jumped up and scrambled toward the other end of the car. The laborer aimed a kick at the retreating

[1] A laborer is someone who does rough work, like digging ditches.

back of the old woman but missed as she scuttled to safety. This so enraged the drunk that he grabbed the metal pole in the center of the car and tried to wrench it out of its stanchion. I could see that one of his hands was cut and bleeding. The train lurched ahead, the passengers frozen with fear. I stood up.

I was young then, some twenty years ago, and in pretty good shape. I'd been putting in a solid eight hours of Aikido training nearly every day for the past three years. I liked to throw and grapple. I thought I was tough. The trouble was, my martial skill was untested in actual combat. As students of Aikido, we were not allowed to fight.

"Aikido," my teacher had said again and again, "is the art of reconciliation. Whoever has the mind to fight has broken his connection with the universe. If you try to dominate people, you are already defeated. We study how to resolve conflict, not how to start it."

I listened to his words. I tried hard. I even went so far as to cross the street to avoid the *chimpira,* the pinball punks who lounged around the train stations. My forbearance exalted me. I felt both tough and holy. In my heart, however, I wanted an absolutely legitimate opportunity whereby I might save the innocent by destroying the guilty.

"This is it!" I said to myself as I got to my feet. "People are in danger. If I don't do something fast, somebody will probably get hurt."

Seeing me stand up, the drunk recognized a chance to focus his rage. "Aha!" he roared. "A foreigner! You need a lesson in Japanese manners."

I held on lightly to the commuter strap overhead and gave him a slow look of disgust and dismissal. I planned to take this turkey apart, but he had to make the first move. I wanted him mad, so I pursed my lips and blew him an insolent kiss.

"All right!" he hollered. "You're gonna get a lesson." He gathered himself for a rush at me.

A fraction of a second before he could move, someone shouted "Hey!" It was earsplitting. I remember the strangely joyous, lilting quality of it—as though you and a friend had been searching diligently for something, and he had suddenly stumbled upon it, "Hey!"

I wheeled to my left; the drunk spun to his right. We both stared down at a little, old Japanese man. He must have been well into his seventies, this tiny gentleman, sitting there immaculate in his kimono. He took no notice of me, but beamed delightedly at the laborer, as though he had a most important, most welcome secret to share.

"C'mere," the old man said in an easy vernacular, beckoning to the drunk. "C'mere and talk with me." He waved his hand slightly.

The big man followed, as if on a string. He planted his feet belligerently in front of the old gentleman, and roared above the clacking wheels, "Why the hell should I talk to you?" The drunk now had his back to me. If his elbow moved so much as a millimeter, I'd drop him in his socks.

The old man continued to beam at the laborer. "Whatcha been drinkin'?" he asked, his eyes sparkling with interest. "I been drinkin' *sake*," the laborer bellowed back, "and it's none of your business!" Flecks of spittle spattered the old man.

"Oh, that's wonderful," the old man said, "absolutely wonderful! You see, I love *sake* too. Every night, me and my wife (she's 76, you know), we warm up a little bottle of sake and take it out into the garden, and we sit on an old wooden bench. We watch the sun go down, and we look to see how our persimmon tree is doing. My great-grandfather planted that tree, and we worry about whether it will recover from those ice storms we had last winter. Our tree has done better than I expected, though, especially when you consider the poor quality of the soil. It is gratifying to watch when we take our *sake* and go out to enjoy the evening—even when it rains!" He looked up at the laborer, eyes twinkling.

As he struggled to follow the old man's conversation, the drunk's face began to soften. His fists slowly unclenched. "Yeah," he said. "I love persimmons, too. . . ." His voice trailed off.

"Yes," said the old man, smiling, "and I'm sure you have a wonderful wife."

"No," replied the laborer. "My wife died." Very gently, swaying with the motion of the train, the big man began to sob. "I don't got no *wife*, I don't got no *home*, I don't got no *job*. I'm so *ashamed* of myself." Tears rolled down his cheeks; a spasm of despair rippled through his body.

Now it was my turn. Standing there in my well-scrubbed youthful innocence, my make-this-world-safe-for-democracy righteousness, I suddenly felt dirtier than he was.

Then the train arrived at my stop. As the doors opened, I heard the old man cluck sympathetically. "My, my," he said, "that is a difficult predicament, indeed. Sit down here and tell me about it."

I turned my head for one last look. The laborer was sprawled on the seat, his head in the old man's lap. The old man was softly stroking the filthy, matted hair.

As the train pulled away, I sat down on a bench. What I had wanted to do with muscle had been accomplished with kind words. I had just seen Aikido tried in combat, and the essence of it was love. I would have to practice the art with an entirely different spirit. It would be a long time before I could speak about the resolution of conflict.

MARY FISHER

By Elinor Briggs and Elizabeth Yeats

Setting: Mary Fisher was an uneducated woman of thirty when she heard George Fox speak. His message changed her life and gave her courage she would never have dreamed she had.

When you are doing housework, your hands are busy but your mind has lots of time to think," thought Mary Fisher as she folded the laundry. "I need to think about what that Quaker, George Fox, said last night!"

Mary was a young woman who had worked hard as a maid for a wealthy family for several years. She was grateful that they were kind to her. They were deeply religious people who encouraged her to hear traveling ministers.

As she sorted the clothes into piles, she wondered at the words she had heard the night before. "Turn to your Inward Teacher, Jesus Christ," George Fox had said. "Everyone can follow him and do the Lord's work."

"Everyone?" thought Mary. "Even a serving maid?"

Mary heard other traveling Quakers after that. Listening to them and meeting with them in silent worship over a period of time, Mary knew that it was true. Even she, a serving maid, *could* hear the Inward Christ. If she listened hard, God *did* tell her what to do. She joined the Quakers and began to follow what God led her to do.

Listening in the silence for God's leadings, she found herself doing things few women in her times would have dared to do. One thing she dared to do soon after she joined the Quakers was to talk about her new religious ideas to her parish priest. For speaking such unusual ideas, she was put in prison in York castle. But in prison she was far from alone. Many Quakers at that time were being imprisoned for teaching about their beliefs. Other Quaker prisoners befriended Mary, taught her how to read and write, and struggled with her to understand that the Lord could set them free in spirit and give them courage to help and teach others, even in prison.

When at last, after many long months, she was released from prison, Mary felt led to start traveling with other Friends to bring word of the Inward Teacher to people all over England and even other countries. Many times she was treated cruelly by government and church officials, but she prayed for those who whipped and imprisoned her, asking God to forgive them.

Sometimes Mary's visits were quite successful. After a long and dangerous voyage across the Atlantic Ocean, Mary and her companion were welcomed on the small island of Barbados, where they taught many people about the Inward Christ.

But when they sailed north to Boston, their welcome was very different. When they arrived, all their possessions were taken from them. Their books were burned. Mary and her companions were taken to a prison cell where the window was boarded up so no one would be able to see or talk to them. They would have starved to death had not a kindly man, Nicholas Upsall, bribed a guard to let him provide food. They prayed that the government officials would let them talk to the people of the Massachusetts Colony, but the authorities were worried that their ideas might cause trouble in the colony. After five weeks, Mary and her companion were sent back to Barbados, and the captain was warned to bring no more Quakers to Boston.

The most dangerous journey Mary Fisher was led to make was to the Sultan, the ruler of Turkey. Turkey was far from

England, but the Sultan's armies were greatly feared through-out Europe. The Sultan and his officers were considered mean and dangerous men. Mary felt God's leading to bring the message of the Inward Teacher, available to all people, to this young ruler, who had so much power and could cause such violence.

Five other Quakers set out with Mary to visit the Sultan, but because of the risks of the trip and the sincere warnings of British officials along the way that even more danger was ahead, all five companions turned back. Only Mary Fisher reached her destination after a six-hundred mile trip alone, on foot and unarmed, through the mountains of northern Greece.

Arriving in the town outside where the Sultan was camped, she had yet another problem. She could not find an official willing even to suggest to the Sultan that he see her. Everyone knew the Sultan was a dangerous man. If he did not like what Mary Fisher said, he might have her killed—and also the person who had dared to bring her there.

Finally, the Sultan's chief advisor agreed to see Mary Fisher himself. His name was Kupruli, and he was quite old and known to be very cruel. But Mary approached him without fear. It took a long time to persuade him, but finally Kupruli agreed to arrange a meeting with the Sultan the next day.

Since Mary Fisher spoke of herself as a messenger of God, the Sultan prepared to see her as an ambassador. He dressed in cloth of gold with fur trim, and all his counselors and court officials wore their brightly colored robes with rich embroidery. Mary had only her simple, worn travel dress, but she entered the court with confidence and went to her appointed place in front of the Sultan in silence.

But there she remained silent! She was still waiting for God to give her the message she was to speak. The Sultan became confused. He commanded Mary to speak the word of God, the message she had come all that way to bring. Still Mary remained silent, listening for the Inward Voice. Finally, she began to speak, a simple message appealing to that of God in the hearts of her listeners and asking them to look inward to know God for themselves.

When she had finished, the Sultan asked, "Is that the whole message?"

"Yes," answered Mary. "Hast thou understood?"

"Yes, and it was the Truth," was the Sultan's response.

The Sultan offered her an armed escort to take her to the sea, but Mary said, "God hath brought me safely here and will guide me safely back." She said good-bye to the Sultan and his court and made the long and dangerous journey back to England.

Later, Mary Fisher married a Quaker missionary preacher and had several children. After he died at sea, she married John Crosse, who took her to live in Charleston, South Carolina. She lived to be 74 and is buried there in an unmarked grave, following the Quaker custom of that time. Despite two married names, she is almost always remembered as Mary Fisher, the Quaker serving maid who, led by God, made that remarkable journey to speak Truth to the Grand Sultan of Turkey.

Sources for this story included; *A Faith to Live By* by Elfrida Vipont Foulds (Friends General Conference, 1963); *The Valiant Sixty* by Ernest E. Taylor (Bannisdale Press, 1951); *Builders of the Quaker Road* by Caroline Nicholson Jacobs (Regnery, 1953)

JELLY BEANS

By Isabel Champ Wolseley

The four of us were new Christians when we ran across the verse, "If your enemy is hungry, feed him." (Romans 12:20 RSV) during our family Bible reading.

Our sons, seven and ten at the time, were especially puzzled. "Why should you feed your enemy?" they wondered.

My husband and I wondered, too, but the only answer John could think of to give the boys was, "We're supposed to because God says so." It never occurred to us that we would soon learn why by experience.

Day after day John Jr. came home from school complaining about a classmate who sat behind him in fifth grade. "Bob keeps jabbing me when Miss Smith isn't looking. One of these days when we're out on the playground, I'm going to jab him back!"

I was ready to go down to the school and jab Bob myself. Obviously the boy was a brat. Besides, why wasn't Miss Smith doing a better job with her kids? I'd better give her an oral jab, too, at the same time.

I was still stewing and fuming over this injustice to John Jr. when his seven-year-old brother spoke up: "Maybe he should feed his enemy."

Reprinted with the permission of the author.

The three of us were startled.

None of us was sure about this "enemy" business. It didn't seem that an enemy would be in the fifth grade. An enemy was someone who was way off . . . well, somewhere. (Exactly where, however, remained a bit vague.)

We all looked at John, but the only answer he could offer was the same one he had given before: "Because God says so."

"Well, if God says so, you'd better do it," I told John Jr. "Do you know what Bob likes to eat? If you're going to feed him, you may as well get something he likes."

Our elder son thought a moment. "Jelly beans!" he shouted. "Bob just loves jelly beans."

So we bought a bag of jelly beans for him to take to school the next day. We would see whether or not enemy feeding worked.

That night we discussed the strategy to be used. When Bob jabbed John Jr. in the back the next time, John would turn around and deposit the bag of jelly beans on his enemy's desk.

The next afternoon I watched and waited impatiently for the yellow school bus to pull up, then dashed out the door to meet the boys before they got even halfway to the house. John Jr. called ahead, "It worked, Mom! It worked!" His little brother claimed responsibility, "Hey, remember, it was me who thought it up."

I wanted details: "What did Bob do? What did he say?"

"He was so surprised he didn't say anything—he just took the jelly beans. But he didn't jab me the rest of the day!"

Well, it wasn't long before John Jr. and Bob became the best of friends—all because of a little bag of jelly beans.

Both our sons subsequently became missionaries in foreign fields. Their way to show friendship with any "enemies" of the faith was to invite the inhabitants of those countries into their own homes to share food around their own tables.

It seems "enemies" are always hungry. Maybe that's why God said to feed them.

THE SECOND MILE

By Janet Sabina

Setting: This story takes place about two thousand years ago in the time of
Jesus, hundreds of years before there were cars or trucks. Except for a few
people who had a donkey or a camel, people walked where they wanted to
go, and carried water or wood or whatever needed to be carried on their
backs. They were ruled by Rome, a powerful country across the sea. One of
the Roman laws was that any time he wanted to, any Roman soldier could
demand that someone carry his pack for a mile, and the person had to do
it. People hated the Roman soldiers, and they hated that law.

David stepped into the dust beside the road and put down
the firewood he had been gathering. He was almost
home. This would be his last stop to rest.

A heavy hand dropped out of nowhere onto his shoulder.
A rough voice said, "Pick up my pack, Jew. I'm tired." The voice
and the hand belonged to a Roman soldier.

David struggled to swallow a terrible anger. He knew what
would happen if he picked up a piece of his firewood and hit
the soldier with it. Jews were beaten for disobeying Romans.

David saw this soldier's strong leather sandals toe to toe
with his own bare feet. He saw the soldier's hand resting on the
short sword that hung from his belt. The soldier's red cape

Adapted with permission from *The Story Teller in Religious Education*, by Jean-
nette Perkins Brown, The Pilgrim Press, copyright 1951, New York, NY.

billowed out in a gust of wind that blew dust into David's eyes as he looked up at the soldier. He swallowed painfully. There was nothing to do but drop his eyes, leave his firewood, and carry the soldier's pack.

"It's only for a mile," David told himself as he slung the heavy pack over his shoulder and bent his back to take its weight. It was hard to keep up with the soldier, who was striding on ahead. "The law says he can't force me to go one step more than that."

David thought about his firewood. Would it still be there when he got back? "One mile, one mile," made a miserable chant in his mind in time with his steps. "One mile, one mile."

Suddenly, the words brought another picture into his head. He saw a meadow on the side of a hill near his home. He saw himself in a crowd of people who were listening to the amazing man, Jesus, the healer and teacher from Nazareth. That day, Jesus had said something odd about carrying packs for Roman soldiers. "Love your enemies," he had said. "Do good to those who hate you. If someone forces you to go one mile, go with him two."

"Why?" David had thought. "Why carry a soldier's pack twice as far as the law says I must?"

David thought Jesus had bent over a little when he said it, as though he knew how it felt to carry a soldier's pack, and then had straightened up and smiled after he gave this advice. David couldn't understand it.

He was so busy thinking that he did not notice when the soldier stopped at the next mile marker. David almost ran into him.

"You have come a mile," said the soldier. "Give me the pack."

David hesitated. He looked at the soldier's face and saw that he was young and that he was very tired too. David made a decision. "I'll carry your pack to the next marker," he said.

The soldier's eyebrows shot up. "What?" he exclaimed. "Why? Why would you do that?"

"Someone I know suggested it," answered David. "Come on. I want to see what happens."

David and the young soldier walked on, side by side this time. The soldier told David about the far-away places he had seen and how homesick he got. He asked David to tell more about the great healer and teacher, Jesus. They talked about friends and work and home.

When they came to the stone that marked the second mile, they both stopped. David took off the pack and helped adjust it on the soldier's back. The soldier put out his hand. David took it. They looked at each other and smiled. Then each went his own way.

David felt different as he walked back toward home. He felt that two weights were off his shoulders. He didn't have the pack, and he didn't carry the hate either. "It works!" he said to himself. "It works! I walked one mile behind an enemy. Then I walked another mile with a friend."

And to make his day almost perfect, he found his firewood too.

While Jean Valjean and the bishop were talking, the servant laid a silver fork and spoon for the stranger, drew the table nearer to the fire, and, at the bishop's request, replaced the lamp with two lighted candles on large silver candlesticks.

"Monseigneur, you are good," said the man. "You do not despise me, even though I have told you where I come from?"

"No, I do not despise you," answered the bishop gently. "As to this house, when I became a priest, I took vows of poverty. This house is for me to share, and this door does not demand of him who enters whether he has a name, but whether he has a grief. Why do I need to know who you are? Besides, before you told me your name, you had a name that I knew."

"Really? You knew what I was called?"

"Yes," replied the bishop, "you are called my brother."

The supper was placed before them, and the stranger ate hungrily while he told more of his sad story. He had been very poor as a child; later, when he stole money for bread to feed his sister's children, he was put in prison for it. There he had suffered terribly and had become very bitter. The bishop, in turn, told him about relatives in the town to which Jean Valjean was going, and about their great cheese-making industry, suggesting it as a new work that it might be worth while to try.

Soon after supper, the bishop said goodnight to his sister, took one of the silver candlesticks from the table, handed the other to his guest, and said to him, "Sir, may I show you to your room?"

In order to reach the small guest room, they passed through the bishop's bedroom, where at that moment the servant was putting the silver away in a cupboard near the head of the bishop's bed. Very soon, after the bishop had made his guest comfortable, all were asleep in the little house.

As the cathedral clock struck two, Jean Valjean woke up. Perhaps it was the strangeness of sleeping in a real bed that made him do so. For a little while he lay there thinking. One idea kept coming to him again and again. Those silver forks and spoons—the servant had put them away in the bishop's room. If he could sell them, they would bring a lot of money. Something made him hesitate as the intention to steal grew in him, but suddenly he decided to act.

He got up and went to his window. It looked out into the garden, which was lighted dimly by the moon behind the clouds. He stole quietly into the bishop's room, but stopped at the bedside, a little frightened and strangely stirred by the sight of the bishop's face. It was a face so full of joy and peace and perfect trust that it quite amazed him. Never before had he seen anything like this!

For many minutes he stood there, fascinated. Then suddenly he moved forward to the cupboard, found that the key was in the lock, opened the door, and stealthily lifted out the basket of silver. Then he tiptoed quickly back to his room, put the silver into his knapsack, climbed out of the window into the garden, nimbly scaled the garden wall, and hurried away.

The next morning at sunrise, as the bishop was walking in his garden, his sister came hurrying to him. "Monseigneur," she cried, "the man has gone and the silver has been stolen!"

The bishop was silent for a moment. Then he said gently, "And in the first place, was that silver ours, Sister? I have for a long time kept that silver wrongfully. A priest should own nothing. The silver belongs to the poor. Who was that man? A poor man, it seems."

A few moments later, as they were eating breakfast, there came a knock at the door.

"Come in," said the bishop, as always.

The door was opened. Outside were five men. Three were policemen, one holding Jean Valjean by the collar. The fifth man, who seemed to be in charge, entered and approached. But the bishop had already stepped quickly toward them.

"Ah, here you are!" he exclaimed, looking at Jean Valjean. "I am glad to see you. But how is this? The candlesticks are yours too. They are of silver like the rest. Why did you not carry them away with your forks and spoons?"

Jean Valjean opened his eyes wide and stared at the bishop with an expression that is impossible to describe.

"So, then," said the officer, "what this man said is true? We found him walking like a man who is running away. He had this silver. . . ."

"And he told you," interrupted the bishop with a smile, "that it had been given to him by a kindly old fellow of a priest with whom he had spent the night. I see how the matter stands. And so you brought him back here. I thank you, but it has been a mistake."

"In that case," said the officer, "we can let him go?"

"Certainly," said the bishop, "and you may leave us. I thank you for your trouble."

The policeman let go of Jean Valjean, and the men left, with apologies. Jean Valjean remained in the doorway, looking bewildered.

"My friend," continued the bishop, "here are your candlesticks. Take them." He stepped to the chimney piece, took down the two candlesticks, and brought them to Jean Valjean, who was trembling all over.

"By the way," added the bishop, "It is not necessary to pass through the garden. You can always enter and depart through the street door. It is never locked."

Jean Valjean looked as if he felt faint.

"Do not forget, my friend, that you have promised to use this money in becoming an honest man."

Jean Valjean, who had no recollection of having promised any such thing, remained speechless. The bishop went on, "Jean Valjean, my brother, you no longer belong to evil but to good."

That moment touched Jean Valjean's heart as no other moment ever had. He looked long at the bishop's kindly face, then tried to mumble a "Thank you" as he turned to go. With the silver candlesticks tucked safely in his knapsack, he closed the door behind him, more gently than he had opened it the afternoon before. And indeed, he lived a life of love and generosity to all he met from that day on.

THANK YOU, M'AM

By Langston Hughes

She was a large woman with a large purse that had everything in it but a hammer and nails. It had a long strap, and she carried it slung across her shoulder. It was about eleven o'clock at night, dark, and she was walking alone, when a boy ran up behind her and tried to snatch her purse. The strap broke with a sudden single tug the boy gave it from behind. But the boy's weight and the weight of the purse combined caused him to lose his balance. Instead of taking off full blast as he had hoped, the boy fell on his back on the sidewalk and his legs flew up. The large woman simply turned around and kicked him right square in his blue-jeaned sitter. Then she reached down, picked the boy up by his shirt front, and shook him till his teeth rattled.

After that the woman said, "Pick up my pocketbook, boy, and give it here."

She still held him tightly. But she bent down enough to permit him to stoop and pick up her purse. Then she said, "Now ain't you ashamed of yourself?"

Firmly gripped by his shirt front, the boy said, "Yes'm."

The woman said, "What did you want to do it for?"

The boy said, "I didn't aim to."

She said, "You a lie!"

By that time two or three people passed, stopped, turned to look, and some stood watching.

"If I turn you loose, will you run?" asked the woman.

"Yes'm," said the boy.

"Then I won't turn you loose," said the woman. She did not release him.

"Lady, I'm sorry," whispered the boy.

"Um-hum! Your face is dirty. I got a great mind to wash your face for you. Ain't you got nobody home to tell you to wash your face?"

"No'm," said the boy.

"Then it will get washed this evening," said the large woman, starting up the street, dragging the frightened boy behind her.

He looked as if he were fourteen or fifteen, frail and willow-wild, in tennis shoes and blue jeans.

The woman said, "You ought to be my son. I would teach you right from wrong. Least I can do right now is to wash your face. Are you hungry?"

"No'm," said the being-dragged boy. "I just want you to turn me loose."

"Was I bothering *you* when I turned that corner?" asked the woman.

"No'm."

"But you put yourself in contact with *me*," said the woman. "If you think that that contact is not going to last awhile, you got another thought coming. When I get through with you, sir, you are going to remember Mrs. Luella Bates Washington Jones."

Sweat popped out on the boy's face and he began to struggle. Mrs. Jones stopped, jerked him around in front of her, put a half nelson about his neck, and continued to drag him up the street. When she got to her door, she dragged the boy inside, down a hall, and into a large kitchenette-furnished room at the rear of the house. She switched on the light and left the door open. The boy could hear other roomers laughing and talking in the large house. Some of their doors were open, too, so he knew he and the woman were not alone. The woman still had him by the neck in the middle of her room.

She said, "What is your name?"

"Roger," answered the boy.

"Then, Roger, you go to that sink and wash your face," said the woman, whereupon she turned him loose—at last. Roger looked at the door—looked at the woman—looked at the door— *and went to the sink.*

"Let the water run till it gets warm," she said. "Here's a clean towel."

"You gonna take me to jail?" asked the boy, bending over the sink.

"Not with that face, I would not take you nowhere," said the woman. "Here I am trying to get home to cook me a bit to eat, and you snatch my pocketbook! Maybe you ain't been to your supper either, late as it be. Have you?"

"There's nobody home at my house," said the boy.

"Then we'll eat," said the woman. "I believe you're hungry— or been hungry—to try to snatch my pocketbook!"

"I want a pair of blue suede shoes," said the boy.

"Well, you didn't have to snatch *my* pocketbook to get some suede shoes," said Mrs. Luella Bates Washington Jones. "You could of asked me."

"M'am?"

The water dripping from his face, the boy looked at her. There was a long pause. A very long pause. After he had dried his face and not knowing what else to do, dried it again, the boy turned around, wondering what next. The door was open. He could make a dash for it down the hall. He could run, run, *run!*

The woman was sitting on the day bed. After a while she said, "I were young once and I wanted things I could not get."

There was another long pause. The boy's mouth opened. Then he frowned, not knowing he frowned.

The woman said, "Um-hum! You thought I was going to say *but*, didn't you? You thought I was going to say, but I didn't snatch people's pocketbooks. Well, I wasn't going to say that." Pause. Silence. "I have done things, too, which I would not tell you, son—neither tell God, if He didn't already know. Everybody's got something in common. So you set down while I fix us something to eat. You might run that comb through your hair so you will look presentable."

In another corner of the room behind a screen was a gas plate and an icebox. Mrs. Jones got up and went behind the screen. The woman did not watch the boy to see if he was going to run now, nor did she watch her purse, which she left behind her on the day bed. But the boy took care to sit on the far side of the room, away from the purse, where he thought she could easily see him out of the corner of her eye if she wanted to. He did not trust the woman *not* to trust him. And he did not want to be mistrusted now.

"Do you need somebody to go to the store," asked the boy, "maybe to get milk or something?"

"Don't believe I do," said the woman, "unless you just want sweet milk yourself. I was going to make cocoa out of this canned milk I got here.

"That will be fine," said the boy.

She heated some lima beans and ham she had in the icebox, made the cocoa, and set the table. The woman did not ask the boy anything about where he lived, or his folks, or anything else that would embarrass him. Instead, as they ate, she told him about her job in a hotel beauty shop that stayed open late, what the work was like, and how all kinds of women came in and out, blondes, redheads, and Spanish. Then she cut him a half of her ten-cent cake.

"Eat some more, son," she said.

When they were finished eating, she got up and said,"Now here, take this ten dollars and buy yourself some blue suede shoes. And next time, do not make the mistake of latching onto my pocketbook *nor anybody else's*—because shoes got by devilish ways will burn your feet. I got to get my rest now. But from here on in, son, I hope you will behave yourself."

She led him down the hall to the front door and opened it. "Good night! Behave yourself, boy!" she said, looking out into the street as he went down the steps.

The boy wanted to say something other than "Thank you, M'am," to Mrs. Luella Bates Washington Jones, but although his lips moved, he couldn't even say that as he turned at the foot of the barren stoop and looked up at the large woman in the door. Then she shut the door.

THE PUNISHMENT
THAT NEVER CAME

By Janet Sabina

An old man with the old-fashioned name of Rufus Jones wondered about something important. "How did my parents help me know God from inside myself instead of just knowing what *other* people said about God?" he asked himself. An answer came.

Rufus remembered a hot summer day when he was a boy. He had done something wrong and expected to be punished. He remembered what happened instead.

Young Rufus wasn't very big, but he was old enough for his parents to leave him alone on the farm while they went to town. He was pleased to be trusted not to get into trouble, to take care of himself with no adult close by.

"We'll be gone several hours, Rufus," said his mother. "We expect you to dig the weeds out of the turnip garden while we're gone. Turnips need space. They won't grow big and tasty if weeds choke them."

"OK," answered Rufus. "I'll weed the turnip patch while you're gone."

Based on an incident recounted in *Friend of Life* by Elizabeth Gray Vining, J.B. Lippincott, 1958.

Rufus meant to keep his promise. He started the job, but before long two of his friends came by on their way to go fishing.

"Come with us," they urged.

"Can't," said Rufus. "Gotta dig these weeds."

"How about if we help you on the way back?" one of the friends suggested. "It'll be cooler by then. It's too hot to work now."

Rufus hadn't felt especially hot until then. But now he felt the sweat on his face and felt his clothes sticking to him. The more he thought about it, the more he liked the idea of waiting till later to do the work and having help.

Off went the three boys. They had so much fun fishing and then swimming afterwards that they stayed much longer than Rufus had expected. When they got back, Rufus' parents were just getting home too.

"But they didn't punish me or even scold me," he remembered. "Mother took me by the hand and didn't let go until she led me to my room and put me in a chair there. Then she knelt down by the bed and started to talk to God about me.

"She told God all about me, what kind of a boy I was, good and bad, and what kind of a man she hoped I'd be. She had big hopes for me, big dreams. At the end, she said, 'O God, take this boy of mine and help him to become the man he was divinely designed to be.'

"Then she just kissed me and left me alone in the silence with God.

"That was the day I started to hear God from inside myself. That was the day."

CHRISTMAS DAY
IN THE MORNING

By Pearl S. Buck

Setting: Rob was fifteen and lived on a farm. Every morning he had to drag himself out of bed at 4 AM to help with the milking. Sometimes he thought he just couldn't do it.

Rob loved his father. He had not known how much until one day a few days before Christmas when he had overheard what his father was saying to his mother.

"Mary, I hate to call Rob in the mornings. He's growing so fast and needs his sleep. I wish I could manage alone."

"Well, you can't, Adam." His mother's voice was brisk.

"I know," his father said slowly, "but I sure do hate to wake him."

When he heard these words, something in him woke: his father loved him! He had never thought of it before. He got up quicker after that, stumbling blind with sleep, and pulled on his clothes, his eyes tight shut, but he got up.

And then on the night before Christmas, that year when he was fifteen, he lay on his side and looked out of his attic window. He wished he had a better present for his father than a ten-cent store tie.

The stars were bright outside, and one star in particular was so bright that he wondered if it were really the Star of Bethlehem. "Dad," he had once asked, "What is a stable?"

"It's just a barn," his father had replied, "like ours."

Then Jesus had been born in a barn, and to a barn the shepherds and the wise men had come, bringing their Christmas gifts.

The thought struck him like a silver dagger. Why should he not give his father a special gift? He could get up early, earlier than four o'clock, and he could creep out to the barn and get the milking done. He'd do it alone—milk and clean up, and then when his father went in to start the milking, he'd see it all done. And he would know who had done it.

He must have waked twenty times during the night. At a quarter to three he got up and put on his clothes. He crept downstairs, careful of the creaky boards, and let himself out. A big star hung over the barn roof, a reddish gold. The cows looked at him, sleepy and surprised.

He had never milked alone before, but it seemed almost easy. He kept thinking about his father's surprise. He smiled and milked steadily, two strong streams rushing into the pail, frothing and fragrant. The cows were still surprised but acquiescent. For once they were behaving well, as though they knew it was Christmas.

The task went more easily than ever before. Milking for once was not a chore. It was something else, a gift for a father who loved him.

Back in his room, he had only a minute to pull off his clothes in the darkness and jump into bed, for he heard his father up. He put the covers over his head to silence his quick breathing. The door opened.

"Rob!" his father called. "We have to get up, son, even if it's Christmas."

"Aw-right," he said sleepily.

"I'll go on out," his father said. "I'll get things started."

The door closed and he lay still, laughing to himself. The minutes were endless—ten, fifteen, he did not know how many—and he heard his father's footsteps again.

"Rob!"

"Yes, Dad—"

His father was laughing, a queer, sobbing sort of a laugh. "Thought you'd fool me, did you?"

"It's for Christmas, Dad!"

His father sat on the bed and clutched him in a great hug. It was dark, and they could not see each others' faces.

"Son, I thank you. Nobody ever did a nicer thing—"

"Oh, Dad." He did not know what to say. His heart was bursting with love.

"Well, I reckon I can go back to bed," his father said after a moment. "No. Listen—the little ones are waking up. Come to think of it, son, I've never seen you children when you first saw the Christmas tree. I was always in the barn. Come on!"

He got up and pulled on his clothes again and they went down to the Christmas tree, and soon the sun was creeping up to where the star had been. Oh, what a Christmas, and how his heart nearly burst again with shyness and pride as his father told his mother and made the younger children listen about how he, Rob, had got up all by himself.

"The best Christmas gift I have ever had, and I'll remember it, son, every year on Christmas morning, so long as I live."

MY SON! MY SON!

By Mary Esther McWhirter
and Janet Sabina

In-Ho-Oh finished a letter to his mother and father in Korea. He knew they missed him. They were proud that he was a college student in the United States, but they missed him. They waited for his letters.

He signed his name and slipped the letter into an envelope. He had just enough stamps to send it to the city of Pusan in far-off Korea. He had just enough time to put it in the mailbox outside his apartment building before the mail truck was due. He hurried down the steps and into the dark street. As the letter dropped from his hand into the mailbox, he heard someone behind him whisper, "Him."

The whisper came from one of eleven teenage boys who were waiting in the dark. They wanted to go to a dance, but they had no money. They were waiting for someone to rob. They chose In-Ho-Oh.

The attack was over in a few terrible seconds. In-Ho-Oh died in a city hospital soon after he was brought there. His life was over. His parents would soon receive the last letter they would every have from their much loved son.

Based on clippings from *The Evening Bulletin* and *The Philadelphia Inquirer,* Spring 1958.

The newspapers of Philadelphia, where this happened, carried the story of the murder on the front page. When the boys who had robbed and killed In-Ho-Oh were caught, people demanded that they pay the greatest penalty for their crime. They demanded the death penalty.

In the midst of the news stories and anger in Philadelphia came a letter from Korea. It was from the mother and father of In-Ho-Oh. The letter asked that the boys who had murdered their son be given "the most lenient treatment consistent with the laws of your government." In-Ho-Oh's mother and father did not want the hardest punishment. They asked for the least!

"We are not very rich people, by any means," the letter went on to say. "In fact, we could not even send money to our son very often, and he had to work to pay his way in college. We regret now that we were not able to help our son more.

"So we want to have someone whom we can help now. Our family is gathering a fund to pay for the religious, educational, vocational, and social guidance of these young men when they are released from jail. We want to turn our sorrow into Christian purpose.

"May God bless you, your people, and particularly the boys who killed our son." The letter was signed Ki-Byung-Oh (his father) and Shin-Hyun-A-Oh (his mother).

Imagine what the people who read this letter thought. Imagine what people who were shouting for the death penalty for the boys must have thought. Here were In-Ho-Oh's parents showing that they had hearts big enough to care about the boys who had killed their only son. They believed God has a heart like that, too. Imagine that.

THE GIANT WHO WAS
MORE THAN A MATCH

A Fable by Aaron Piper

O nce in the land of Kanifloria there lived a man so wise that no one could say just how wise he was. He was also very old—so old that no one could remember his name; and in fact, he had forgotten it himself. So he was simply called the Wise One. The Wise One led a modest life, dwelling in a tiny cottage in a dense forest. Here he nourished himself on wild fruit and nuts and spent long hours meditating deeply or conversing with the trees and forest animals.

Though the Wise One's hermitage was secluded, it lay not too far from the Capital City of Kanifloria. And through another part of the forest ran the only road between the Capital City and the City of Trade. Of course, this was an important road, carrying many travelers and the carts of peddlers and wealthy merchants.

One morning, when the first cart driver from the Capital City had come halfway on his journey, he came upon a giant standing in the middle of the road. The giant barred the way and said, "You shall not pass without fighting me. Choose any weapon you like, and I will more than match you."

Reprinted with permission of *Friends Journal*, © May 1984.

Well, this cart driver was no warrior. He hastily turned his cart around and fled back to the Capital City, warning all the other cart drivers and travelers he met coming along the road. And the same thing happened to the first cart driver from the City of Trade.

It was not long before the President of Kanifloria heard of this. He sent for his Council of Three and asked, "What is your advice in this matter?"

The First Councilor said, "We have a duty to protect the people and maintain their right to travel where they wish. Therefore, one of our warriors must battle the giant. Send the Master of Clubs." So the President called for the Master of Clubs to battle the giant.

The Master of Clubs set out walking the next morning, and in a few hours reached the place where the giant stood. The giant bellowed, "You shall not pass without fighting me. Choose any weapon you like, and I will more than match you."

The warrior called out, "I choose clubs," and lifted up the great oaken club he carried. But no sooner had he done so, than out of nowhere appeared a club in the giant's hands, longer and heavier than the warrior's own. Before the Master of Clubs could even shout again, there was no more left of him than a puddle on the road.

The same thing happened when the President sent the Master of Swords. When he came to the place where the giant stood, the giant roared, "You shall not pass without fighting me. Choose any weapon and I will more than match you."

The warrior shouted, "I choose swords," and raised his blade of polished steel. But no sooner had he done so, than a sword longer and shinier and sharper appeared in the giant's hands. Within seconds, the Master of Swords lay in ribbons on the road.

It was the same with the Master of Fire, their most powerful warrior. He began tossing lit torches at the giant, one after another, almost faster than the eye could see. But as fast as the warrior could throw them, the giant caught them and threw them back even faster, burning brighter and hotter than before.

Within moments, there was nothing but a pile of ashes where the Master of Fire had stood.

The President was now at his wits' end. The President's wife, who was sitting with them, then spoke gently to her husband. "Why not send for the Wise One? Perhaps he can help."

The President said, "What could the Wise One do that our finest warriors could not?"

But since none of them had a better idea, he sent his Councilors to the cottage of the Wise One to speak with him. The Wise One listened quietly to their story. Then he said, "Return to the capital. I will see what can be done."

The next morning the Wise One set off. . . . On the way he stopped at the home of a farmer and borrowed a cart, and a cow to pull it. Riding in this fashion, he reached the road and finally came to the place where the giant stood.

Again the giant roared. "You shall not pass without fighting me. Choose any weapon you like, and I will more than match you."

"Well!" said the Wise One. "I shall have to think on this!" So saying, he settled himself down to ponder. The giant too sat down to think.

After awhile, it came time for the cow to be milked. The Wise One took a pail from the cart, and crouched down beside the cow. When the pail was full, he dipped a cup into the milk, and took a long, deep drink. The giant looked on longingly.

"Could it be that you are thirsty?" said the Wise One.

The giant said, "I admit that I am."

The Wise One filled the cup again with milk, and held it out to the giant. "Please accept this small gift from your humble friend," he said.

"Aha!" cried the giant, leaping up. "Now I see your trick! You seek to conquer me with kindness! But now I will more than match you!"

The giant rushed off and returned within seconds, his arms laden with food: fresh brown bread, figs, buttermilk, dates, olives, cheeses, cherries, everything that someone like the Wise One could have desired. All this he spread out before the Wise One.

"You see you cannot defeat me so easily!" the giant said.

"Yes, so I see!" said the Wise One, settling himself down to the sumptuous meal.

When the Wise One had eaten enough to satisfy his hunger, and a little more, he said to the giant, "I should like you to know something of me. Though I make no such claim for myself, others call me the Wise One. I live in this same forest, not far from the Capital City.

The giant bellowed, "Another of your tricks! Very well, you shall know even more of me than I know of you! I have no name, for I was born of the union of the wind and a curved mirror. And I have no power or skill but what my opponent chooses for me!"

"I thought as much," said the Wise One. "But now the sun is nearly down, and I must reach the City of Trade before dark. . . . May I offer you a ride to a place of rest?"

The giant shrieked. "Yet again you try to trick me! Will you never have done with it? But this time I will defeat you once and for all!"

With that, the giant picked up the Wise One, the cart, and the cow and, holding them all in his arms, ran like the wind all the way to the City of Trade.

When they had reached the city gate, the giant set them down. "I hope you have learned your lesson," he said.

"Oh, I have," said the Wise One. "And I thank you. . . ."

"No," screamed the giant, "Thank *you*—VERY MUCH!" And the giant turned and ran back down the road, vanishing from sight within seconds.

Then the Wise One entered the city, where he explained to the people the nature of the giant, and how they should approach him. And from that day for as long as the giant lived—at least a hundred years—travelers between the two cities had only to bring themselves half the way, for the giant would carry them the rest.

NEGLECT THE FIRE AND YOU CANNOT PUT IT OUT

By Leo Tolstoy

There once lived in a Russian village a peasant named Ivan. He was well off. He was the best worker in the village, and he had three healthy sons who were good workers too. His old father was the only one in the family who was not able to do anything, and they took good care of him. They had all they wanted to eat and wear, and would have been happy had it not been for Ivan's neighbor, Gavrilo the Lame. For Ivan and Gavrilo hated each other.

Once they had been good friends. Then a little thing happened—such a foolish little thing! A hen belonging to Ivan's daughter laid an egg in Gavrilo's yard. Every day this hen had laid an egg in her own shed, and when the daughter heard her cackle, she would go out and get the egg; but this time boys frightened the hen and she flew over the fence. Ivan's daughter was busy that day and did not go for the egg until evening. Then she could not find it, and the boys told her where to look. So she went to her neighbor and met Gavrilo's mother.

"What is it you want, young woman?"

Adapted by Frances M. Dadmun in *Living Together,* The Beacon Press, 1915, pp. 102-107. Used by permission of the publisher.

"Granny, my hen has been in your yard today—did she not lay an egg there?"

The old woman thought that Ivan's daughter was accusing her of taking the egg, so she answered crossly.

"I have not set eyes on her. We have hens of our own, and they have been laying for quite a while. We have gathered our own eggs, and we do not need other people's eggs. Young woman, we do not need to go to other people's yards to gather eggs."

Ivan's daughter did not like this. She replied sharply and Gavrilo's mother answered still more sharply. Ivan's wife came by carrying water; Gavrilo's wife stepped out of her door, and they were all talking at once, scolding and calling each other names. Then the men came up to take the part of their wives and began to hit each other. And Ivan, who was the stronger, hurt Gavrilo the Lame.

Gavrilo took the case to the village court, declaring that he would have Ivan punished. When Ivan's father heard of it, he spoke firmly.

"Children, you are doing a foolish thing. Think of it! The whole affair began from an egg. One egg isn't worth much. There should be enough for everybody. You have said too many cross words; now show them how to say kind ones. Go and make peace, and let there be an end to it. If you keep it up, it will get worse and worse."

But Ivan and his family did not listen. They thought the old man was talking nonsense. Instead of making peace, Ivan went to the court himself and tried to get Gavrilo punished for tearing his shirt when they quarreled over the egg.

After that, the neighbors quarreled every day and always over some foolish thing. They went to court so often that the judge was tired of seeing them coming. And so it went on for six years.

At last, Ivan's daughter accused Gavrilo in public of stealing horses, and Gavrilo struck her so that she was sick for a week. This time it was more serious, and when Ivan took the case to court the judge ordered that Gavrilo be whipped; for this was one of their ways of punishing men who did wrong—and it always hurt very much. When Gavrilo heard what was to be done to him, he turned so white and muttered so angrily that even the judge was alarmed and begged Ivan to forgive him and withdraw the case. But Ivan would not, and went home to tell his father that Gavrilo was to be punished at last.

"Ivan," said the old man, "you are not doing right. You see his badness, but you forget your own. Jesus taught us something quite different. If a cross word is said to you, keep quiet. If they box your ears, turn the other cheek. Make peace with him. It is not too late to stop his being punished, and then you can invite him and his family to dinner."

Then, when Ivan did not start at once, his father added, "Go now, Ivan. Your anger is like fire. Put it out at the start, for when it burns hotly you cannot control it."

Ivan began to see what his father meant. He was ready to go and make peace, when the women came in and said that Gavrilo was so angry that he had threatened to set fire to the house. Then Ivan grew hot again, just as if he were on fire himself, and would not stop Gavrilo's punishment.

That night, Ivan remembered what Gavrilo had said about setting a fire, and he was so troubled that he went out to examine the yard. He walked softly along by the fence. He had just turned the corner when it seemed to him that something stirred at the other end, as though it had got up and sat down again. Ivan stopped and stood still—he listened and looked; everything was quiet, only the wind rustled the leaves in the willow tree and crackled through the straw. It was pitch-dark, but his eyes got used to the darkness. He stood and looked, but there was no one there.

"It must have only seemed so to me," said Ivan, "but I will go and see."

He stepped so softly that he could not hear his own footsteps. He came to the corner and stopped. He could clearly see someone in a cap squatting down with his back toward him, and setting fire to a bunch of straw in his hands. He stood stock-still.

"Now," he thought, "he will not get away from me. I will catch him on the spot."

Then it grew bright. The flame licked up the straw in the shed and leaped to the roof. It was no longer a small fire. Gavrilo showed plainly in the light of it. Ivan made a rush for him, but Gavrilo got away and, lame as he was, ran like a hare. Ivan, however, overtook him and caught him by the skirt of his coat, but the skirt tore off and Ivan fell down and hurt his head. When he got up, Gavrilo was gone. It was light as day, and Ivan could hear the roaring and crackling in his yard. Then he saw the burning straw from the shed being blown toward the house.

Ivan tried to get there to stop it. "If I could only pull the straw out of the shed and put out the fire!" he thought. But his feet would not move at all, at first. Then they tripped each other up. People came running, but nothing could be done. The neighbors dragged their own things out of their houses and drove out the cattle. After Ivan's house, Gavrilo's caught fire; a wind rose and carried the fire across the street. Half the village burned down.

All they saved from Ivan's house was his old father who had fled to a distant part of the village. When Ivan went to see him, the old man said, "What did I tell you, Ivan? Who burned the village?"

"He did, Father," said Ivan. "I caught him at it. If I could only have seized the burning bunch of straw and pulled it out, it wouldn't have happened."

"Ivan," said his father again, "who was really to blame?"

Ivan stared. Then he remembered how he had hurt Gavrilo in the first place—and how he had not gone to make the peace with him while there was yet time.

"I was to blame, Father," said he. Then Ivan was silent.

After a minute, the old man said, "Ivan."

"Yes, Father."

"What is to be done now?"

"I do not know, Father. How am I to get on? Everything I had is burned."

"You will get along. With God's aid, you will get along. But remember, Ivan, you must not tell anyone that Gavrilo started the fire. If you do not tell, God will forgive you both."

Ivan did not tell and nobody found out how the fire started.

Then Ivan began to feel sorry for Gavrilo. And Gavrilo, in turn, was surprised because Ivan did not tell. At first he was afraid of Ivan, but after a little, he got used to him. The men stopped quarreling and so did their families. While they were rebuilding, they lived together in one house, and when the village was built again, Ivan and Gavrilo were still neighbors. After that, they were always friendly.

Ivan never forgot what his father had told him about putting out the fire at the beginning. If a person spoke sharply to him, he answered kindly. Then the person was ashamed, and there was no quarrel. So Ivan was happier than ever before, and no one in the village had so many friends.

JOHN WOOLMAN

By Elinor Briggs and Elizabeth Yeats

John Woolman was born in 1720, over 250 years ago, on a farm near the Rancocas River, in what is now New Jersey. His family was part of a growing Quaker community struggling to survive in the wilderness. The whole Woolman family—Mother, Father, and all thirteen children—had to pitch in and help each other in every way they could. There were cows to milk, sheep to care for, chickens to feed, the garden to plant and weed, wood to cut, water to carry to the house, and many other things to do.

The Quakers had settled in this spot because they found a good spring for water that the Lenape Indians had been using for years. The Lenape had a burial ground near the spring, and the Quakers felt this was the right place for their cemetery too. They built their meetinghouse close by.

The Quakers also built a small school near the spring. John and his brothers and sisters were never surprised to come into the school and find Lenape Indian children already seated on the benches, ready to learn to read and write. Nor were Friends startled when a head decorated with a tall feather appeared at a meetinghouse window while they were worshiping. The Indians often came in on moccasined feet and joined in the silent worship. John came to know many Lenapes as neighbors and friends.

But John wasn't thinking about Indians or any other of his friends on that day when our story begins. It was a First-Day morning, and the Woolman family was on the way to Meeting for Worship.

"What is a sun worm?" nine-year-old John asked his older sister Elizabeth.

"I have no idea," Elizabeth replied. "Ask Father. He'll know."

John ran ahead to catch up with Father and Mother. They were on horseback, Mother carrying the baby Uriah, and Father holding little Hannah in front of him. The older children were walking along behind.

"Has thee ever seen a sun worm?" John asked, looking up at his father.

"I know of no such creature," Father answered.

John was really confused now. Maybe in the quiet of worship, he would come to understand. He fell back to walk with the other children, soberly recalling the dream he'd had the night before. The moon had risen in the west and had gone swiftly across the sky to the east. Soon the sun had quickly followed the moon. The sun was so strong that it dried up a blooming tree. Then a "sun worm" appeared, "small of size but full of strength."

When they had settled on the benches in the meeting-house, the men on the right and the women on the left, John thought hard about his dream. Was he like the sun worm? He knew that he, like all God's creatures, was a small part of God's larger plan. Would God make him full of strength? Did God have a special plan for him?

Some time after his dream, John was in the garden weeding the carrots.

"John," called Mother from the house, "will thee carry this to our neighbor for me?"

John came willingly, though his back ached from the weeding. He was always happy to do errands, since he had many friends and there was a good chance he would meet one on the way.

But this day was different, and he met no one. As he walked along, he saw a robin fly up from its nest. John took up some stones and aimed at her. The robin fluttered back and forth until one of the stones struck her and she fell dead. John was pleased with his good aim until he realized the truth of what he had done. He had killed an innocent creature. He bent to look at the poor dead bird.

Then John heard chirping. He looked up and saw several baby robins poking their heads up over the edge of the nest. "Oh, no!" thought John. "That robin was a mother. She wouldn't fly away from my stones because she was protecting her babies." Suddenly, John was very sad.

He knew what he had to do. On his farm there was no time to care for tiny birds, and if he left them in the nest, they would die a slow, painful death from starvation. He climbed the tree and sorrowfully killed each one. All his life he would remember killing that robin family. John seemed to know from that day that he must never again use his strength to take the life of any of God"s creatures.

But there were other lessons to learn.

One spring, when John was older, Father was away at Quaker Yearly Meeting for a week. Before he left, Father told John that as he was the eldest son, Mother would depend on him to do the heavy work.

But somehow, when Father was away, it was easier for John to put off doing the chores and go off to visit his friends or read instead. When his mother asked him to bring in more logs for the fire, he forgot. He went off to be with his friends in town. It fell to Asher, John's younger brother, to get the wood.

Later that evening, John was reading by the fire.

"John, why did thee neglect thy duty?" Mother asked. John didn't answer.

"Will thee please go now and take the leather bucket and bring some water from the river?" asked his mother.

"Asher will do it," answered John.

These were the days when a thrashing in the woodshed was a common punishment for a son who had been disobedient. When Father returned, John was soon called to his side.

"While I was abroad, thy mother reproved thee for a misdeed, and thee made her an undutiful reply," his father reminded him.

Remembering the incident, John was immediately ashamed. No thrashing would have made him feel worse. The incident so troubled him that later he wrote in his journal, "I believe that I do not remember ever again speaking unhandsomely to either of my parents."

But as he grew, John gave his family other worries.

"And then there was the time. . . ." John Woolman was off on one of his famous stories. From the time he was old enough, he would finish his chores quickly and then walk the five miles to the town of Mount Holly. There he could usually find a group of young men ready to see who could tell the funniest story.

The family became concerned about him. They considered reading books a good use of his time, though many young Quakers in those days were forbidden to read anything but religious materials. Loitering on street corners—or worse, in the tavern with his boisterous young friends—was considered to be "foolish jesting" by the Woolman family. John's older sister Elizabeth was particularly concerned. She worried about this "backsliding and vanity."

Then John returned home one afternoon with a high fever.

Elizabeth put him immediately to bed. He was very sick. His mind became confused, and he became sure he was dying. As he started to get better, an unusual thing happened. As he lay quietly, thinking about how wonderful it was to be alive and thanking God for his renewed life, he found that God was calling him, telling him that he should live a life of service and devotion. At the time, John didn't know what that service would be, but he knew he would have to stop spending all his free time hanging around with his friends. Soon he would have to decide what kind of work he would do. And he kept thinking about God's call.

When he was up and about, John started going to Meeting for Worship with eagerness and enthusiasm. There he found inspiration and courage to change his life. Most important for John, who always enjoyed being with people, he found new friends who shared his wish to serve God.

One day, John announced excitedly, "Father, I've been offered work as a shopkeeper by a man in Mount Holly!"

"We have wondered if thee would not seek other employment than farming," his father responded. Father knew there were plenty of other Woolman children to share the workload on the farm. He gave his blessing, and John moved to take his new job.

"Come over to the tavern and join us when you close the shop," John's old friends invited him. He had not been to town for some time, and they were glad to have him back.

"I do not care to join you," John answered softly. He hated to turn away his old friends, but his mind was on new things now, such as pleasing his customers, keeping careful accounts, and being honest in his business dealings. In that way, his employer would profit and so would he.

But worldly things were not his only concern. John was always wondering in what direction God would call him. He was soon to know.

John had grown up knowing that many people owned slaves—even many Quakers. But he himself had known black people only as friends. One morning, his employer entered the shop with an elderly Quaker, who asked that John write a bill of sale for his black slave. John knew how to write deeds, bills of sale, and other legal documents from reading his father's law books. But this was different. John knew this black woman as a friend. Suddenly, it was as though she were no more than a horse, a cat, or a sack of flour, with no way to say how she felt.

John was very troubled. He sat a long time, mending his quill pen, frowning, wondering what to do or say. Finally, he slowly wrote out the legal paper. He felt he had no choice since his employer had made the request.

But as they rose to go, John said gently, "I believe slave-keeping to be inconsistent with the Christian religion." This helped ease his conscience a bit, but he knew that from that time on he would have to refuse such tasks. At first, he was fearful that he would lose his job and make people angry with him. But taking courage from God, he would say gently that it was against his conscience to have any part in selling a fellow human being. He was pleased—and at first surprised—when most people agreed with him and quietly left.

As John Woolman grew into manhood, he realized that God was calling him to do more than refuse to be part of selling slaves. But what was he to do? He decided that first he must know more about the living and working conditions of all slaves. Asking people in his Meeting for their support and prayers, he began to travel both north and south.

During his first trip north, he saw the terrible conditions of slaves arriving by ship from Africa. Slaves came across the Atlantic Ocean lying chained side by side, stacked on platforms one just above the other. John experienced first hand the stench that filled the air and saw the pain and sickness on the faces of these people as they were brought out on the dock and led to the auction block to be sold.

His trips south took him far and wide, through heat, cold, rain, and snow. He slept in fine homes, under bushes, and in frontier cabins. He saw some slaves abused and some treated well. But they were never free. When he could, he would slip coins into the hands of those who had waited on him.

He also made an important discovery. Slavery was a deep, festering sore in the whole society, hurting the owners as well as the slaves. Owners lived useless lives, not working themselves but becoming wealthy by the labor of others. John spoke to them gently, with love, trying to make them see the harm that slavery was causing to everyone.

When he returned home, John was clear that slavery was a terrible wrong against God. But how could he, one young

Quaker man, convince even other Quakers who were used to this way of life?

First, John decided that if he was to have time to work on his concern about slavery, he needed to simplify his own life. He must find a permanent kind of work that would support his new wife and growing family and still allow time for him to travel among Friends speaking about slavery. He discovered that tailoring, making clothes for people, left his mind free to ponder God's word and message and also, along with his small farm and orchard, produced enough income to meet his simple needs.

John Woolman now had time to write a pamphlet about the evils of slavery and to travel in Philadelphia Yearly Meeting and elsewhere to share his concern. Although John was very patient, some Friends continued to buy slaves, even after Philadelphia Yearly Meeting approved a query asking Friends not to engage in the slave trade. John went to Yearly Meeting that fall knowing it would be a difficult time for all. As they gathered before worship, feelings ran high.

In the gathered silence, John felt deeply moved to speak his concern. "The time is now!" he began. With simple words, he called upon those present not to neglect their duty to bring all slaves to freedom through God's love and justice. Many Friends found great truth in his words. Out of that Meeting came a minute telling all Friends to stop buying and keeping slaves. It was a true beginning of the end of the evil practice of keeping slaves among Quakers.

As the years passed, John Woolman found himself called by God to do some very unusual things to show his concern for others. Sometimes the members of his Meeting approved of his actions while at other times, he seemed to some of them a bit crazy. His family worried about him constantly because he was often sick. Inside, he continued to hear God calling him to show in one more way his concern for other creatures on the earth.

This was a time of great misunderstanding and violence between the Native American Indians and the European colonists, who continued to settle farther and farther west, pushing the Indians off their lands. The new lands on which the Indians settled were not as good, and many were forced to give up farming and make their living trapping animals and selling the skins to the Europeans. Often the Europeans paid little for the skins, not enough for the Indians to buy food and clothing for their families. Sometimes things were even worse when the Europeans paid for the skins with rum, which made the Indians sick. In addition, some groups of Europeans signed treaties with the Native Americans that other European groups did not obey. No wonder the Indians became violent. "The White man has created his own danger," thought John Woolman.

John felt led to travel to be with the Indians at Wehaloosing, far to the west along the Susquehanna River. His Monthly Meeting tried to talk him out of this long and dangerous trip. "Don't go now!" they said. "There are too many raids on settlements right now." But John knew that a recent treaty had caused much misunderstanding. He must go now, and he must go alone so no one else would be in danger. But when he joined his Native American guide, a young Friend, Benjamin Parvin, was there too. Bejamin Parvin also felt called by God to risk the dangerous trip.

John Woolman was grateful for this young man's company as they traveled the grueling miles of wilderness, crossing rivers and mountains. People they met going the other way would often warn them, "Pontiac, the Indian Chief, is on the war path! Turn back!" At last, they rode up the last hill and met a Wehaloosing woman with a baby on her back. The Wehaloosing had been alerted, she warned them, and the whole village was waiting for them. What would they find?

The guide went into the village first. If John and Benjamin were to follow, he would blow on a conch shell as a sign. They waited in "deep inward silence."

The conch shell sounded, and down into the valley they rode. The camp seemed deserted. They were led into one of the houses, and there, sitting on the ground in gentle silence sat sixty Wehaloosing men. John Woolman recognized some of them. The leader, Papunehang, welcomed them and showed them their places. They sat down and joined in worshiping the Great Spirit.

During the worship, John Woolman was moved to speak. Later, a young man told John Woolman through an interpreter, "I love to feel where the words come from."

"God's message of peace and love has been heard," thought John Woolman, "and trust has been nurtured by my visit." He stayed four days and then felt free to return home.

John resumed his very simple life and continued to devote all his free time to speaking about the evils of slavery. Still he felt God expected him to be doing more. Something about his way of life seemed wrong. For the most part, he no longer used products made by slave lavor. But he did wear clothes and hats colored with dyes made with indigo. He knew that many slaves who worked on indigo plantations died within a few years, poisoned by working with the indigo dye. Would he be serving God best by wearing white, undyed clothes? This would make him look odd at Meeting for Worship, but a few Friends would surely understand.

John decided not to replace all his clothes at once, since throwing away good clothing would be wasteful. As things wore out, he would replace them, one at a time. His hat was worn out right now.

At that time, white hats were the latest fashion for rich young men, so John had no trouble finding one. Wearing it to Meeting was another matter. John was a minister and a well respected member. Imagine Friends' surprise when John walked in wearing his bright white hat. At first, they didn't understand, and John's sensitive spirit suffered. But slowly everyone came to understand that he was wearing undyed clothes to show his love for slaves forced to do work that made them sick. "Besides," said some of his closer friends, "It's so much easier to see him coming as he walks along the roads."

And that was another strange thing John did. He walked a great deal. At first, he walked all over the Chesapeake Bay area in order to understand better the terrible suffering of slaves. "But," he would tell friends, "I can come in out of the hot sun and rest when I get tired, and get water to drink when I am thirsty. Most slaves can't do that. I must do more!"

Finally, John Woolman decided to go to England. Many slaves came to the colonies on English ships, and there were slaves in England also. Friends in London Yearly Meeting could bring pressure on the English government to make laws against these practices. John would bring a minute of concern to London Yearly Meeting from Friends in Philadelphia.

This was not a good time to go to England. In a few years the colonies would be fighting England for their independence, and already there were problems. But John Woolman set his affairs in order and left in early spring on the ocean voyage.

Arriving at the impressive meeting of ministers and elders in London, John slipped quietly in the door and placed his minute on the Clerk's desk. After that, he settled into the nearest seat.

A dead silence followed.

That white hat! Those dowdy, undyed clothes! The English Quakers, in their well-cut, expensive, grey, black, or brown clothes were shocked by what they saw. And Friends in America had asked them to accept this man and even help him in traveling around England!

After a moment of stunned silence, one Friend rose and said that the Friend from America had delivered his minute and could return home. Tears filled John Woolman's eyes, and for a moment he wondered why God had sent him away from his home and dear family at a time when his health was not good, over thousands of miles of ocean. And now he was not to be allowed to finish his mission.

He rose to his feet and told the Meeting that he had not finished the work God had called him to do in England. He would not visit Friends until the Meeting agreed that he should. He knew some trades and would find work and support himself until that time. His words held no anger or resentment. They were words of dedication and love. The silence deepened.

After some time, Woolman rose again and spoke a message that stirred the hearts of all those listening. The Quaker who had suggested that John leave rose again. He admitted his mistake and said he hoped the Friend from America would travel around England delivering his message.

After the Yearly Meeting, John began his travels. Again he was on foot, this time because the horses that pulled the stage coaches in England were often cruelly treated, as were the boys who rode outside, even in freezing weather.

"I'm middling well," he wrote home to his wife and daughter. "I often remember you with tears." But in September of 1772, John Woolman caught small pox. He was completely exhausted from years of hard travel and never recovered. He died in England and was buried there, surrounded by many who loved him.

John Woolman left us a wonderful journal telling us all about his life. But most of all, he left us an example of a life lived constantly seeking to do God's will to bring love and understanding for all God's creatures into the world for all to enjoy.

Sources for this story included: *Builders of the Quaker Road* by Caroline Nicholson Jacobs (Regnery, 1953); *John Woolman, Child of Light* by Catherine Owens Peare (Vanguard Press, 1954); Janet Whitney's editing of Woolman's *Journal* (Regnery, 1950).

SQUANTO

By the Committee

Setting: This is the true story of Squanto, an Algonquian Indian. His full name was Tisquantum. The white men called him Squanto for short.

Squanto's band lived along the shore near Plymouth Rock where the Pilgrims landed. Only it wasn't called Plymouth Rock then, and there weren't any Pilgrims there yet. For Squanto was born about twenty years before the Mayflower came.

Six years before the Pilgrims came, Squanto had grown into a tall young man. One day, as he and his friends roamed the Plymouth coast, an English ship sailed into the harbor. In great excitement, Squanto and several of his friends paddled their canoes out to the big ship. The young men were greatly interested in the strange ship. They carried in their arms piles of furs that they planned to give the white men in exchange for the strange and wonderful wares that English sailors usually brought with them. Captain Hunt invited them aboard and dropped a rope ladder down the side so Squanto and his friends could climb aboard.

The mountain of soft, rich furs that they heaped on the deck represented many months of trapping. But before they

---

Original author unknown. Based on history.

had a chance to begin trading, the captain jerked up the rope ladder. His drawn sword blocked their retreat.

"Tie up the Indians!" he shouted

Squanto struggled wildly as the ropes were drawn tightly around his arms and legs. His pleading did no good. Even as he cried out, other sailors grabbed his companions, binding them in the same way.

The captain's evil intention soon became clear. "We'll sell them in Spain as slaves!" he declared as the anchor was hauled up and the ship floated out to sea.

After several weeks, they sailed into a Spanish harbor where Squanto and his friends were marched down the gangplank and into the village square. There they were sold as slaves and taken away by their new masters.

Not long after that, Squanto managed to escape and was rescued by two Catholic priests. For a time, he stayed with them and worked in their gardens. But they saw that he was homesick. They helped him find a ship that would take him to England, where it would be easier to find a ship to take him back to America.

In London, Squanto met a merchant named John Slanie. The Englishman was very kind to Squanto, never dreaming that a few years later his kindness to the homesick young man would be repaid a thousand times over by Squanto's kindness to the homesick, suffering Pilgrims.

Meanwhile, Squanto's family and band at Plymouth were grieving for him. They attacked every white man who came to their coast. Probably many a sailor who had never thought of kidnapping an Indian was made to suffer for Captain Hunt's cruel act. And then, just three years after Squanto was taken away, a great sickness fell upon the band, and soon hardly an Algonquian Indian was left on the whole Plymouth shore. The few who escaped the plague were afraid to stay there any longer. They just left their buried stores of corn and moved away.

Meanwhile, Squanto, in England, knew nothing of this. He was hoping to see all his people again, for John Slanie had promised to help him go back to America.

The very year before the Mayflower sailed, Squanto did come back. He had been away for five years. He searched the Plymouth shore for his people but found only the empty forest. He trudged forty miles farther to where another band lived. They told him all that had happened. After that, he lived with them, but often he would walk back to Plymouth to look again on the scenes of his childhood.

The next year, the Pilgrims set sail from England. They started too late in the season, and soon the early winter storms were beating upon them, blowing their ship off its course. They were blown five hundred miles north of the place they wanted to land. They were blown right to the shore where Squanto's people had lived.

The Pilgrims landed at Plymouth Rock, as we know. There was the dark forest, stretching before them, strange and silent. The silence frightened them. They imagined the forest full of Indians waiting to attack them. At any moment, they expected to hear the woods ring with a war-whoop. But they heard only the quiet of the winter woods.

Little by little, the settlers, gathering courage, ventured short distances into the forest. No Indians! They found the buried heaps of corn and kept careful count of what they took, so that later they might pay the owners.

Had the Algonquians who once lived there been alive, believing as they did that all white men were wicked kidnappers, they would have destroyed that little Pilgrim company in one swift hour. But there was another enemy—bitter winter—that struck down the Pilgrims, one by one, until by spring half of the little group had died. Food was gone, comfort and health were gone. All but hope was gone. It was a terrible winter.

When spring came, they hardly knew what to do. Just when things were at their worst, Squanto walked into the Pilgrim camp, speaking English. He did not hate them because an English captain had kidnapped him, but wanted to help them because an English merchant had befriended him.

That was a day the Pilgrims long remembered. They wrote it down in their records.

First, Squanto gathered food for them and saved them from starvation. Even more important, he taught them how to find food for themselves, how to plant, how to rig up fish traps, how to fertilize their crops with fish. He made them wise in the ways of animals. He was their ambassador and taught them how to trade with the Indians. For two years he lived with them, their friend and counselor.

After Squanto died, the Pilgrims remembered him lovingly, a man who gave friendship as it had been given to him—instead of the hate he had also been given.

ANNA AND THE SPECKLED HEN

By Ruth Hunt Gefvert

Setting: This story is set in Germany during World War II. Food was scarce; people were malnourished and always hungry, especially children.

Anna was on her weekly trip to the country to try to get food. She had her bicycle, but she was too worn out to ride it, so she was walking along slowly, pushing it. Even that made her heart race. She was tired all the time these days.

She was discouraged, too. Not even the farmers seemed to have any vegetables left. Except for a few beets one man had given her, no one had had anything to give or sell her.

Suddenly, Anna knew she could go no further. She would have to stop and rest. She laid her bicycle on its side, making sure the beets did not spill out of her basket. Then she lay down in the cool grass.

She dreamed of food. All her dreams were about food lately, it seemed. This time she dreamed of carrots the color of gold, steaming hot, in cream and butter. Even in her dream, though, she knew this was foolish, for she could not remember having had either butter or cream. But her mother had told her about

From *Newsletter for Boys and Girls*, American Friends Service Committee. Used by permission of Arthur A. Gefvert.

them, and in her dream she could almost tell how wonderful they tasted.

Next in her dream there were tomatoes, beautiful red, juicy tomatoes. There was a great pile of them, and Anna was just about to eat one when they disappeared. With a start she woke up. She rolled over and sat up. And there, looking her right in the eye, was a speckled hen. They looked at each other—Anna and the hen.

Suddenly, Anna realized the hen was talking. At least she was clucking and making the kind of talk that speckled hens make.

"Why are you staring at me, you silly thing?" asked Anna. "And making all that noise that woke me up," she charged.

"Cu-u-u-t . . . cu-u-u-t . . ." said the hen, startled at Anna's cross-sounding voice, and she backed away.

It was then that Anna saw the egg! Carefully, she picked it up, still warm.

"Oh, you beautiful, beautiful hen!" she exclaimed. "I am sorry I was rude to you. Thank you for this *lovely* egg!"

But the speckled hen had walked off, and Anna was left alone with the egg. She felt better now, more rested. She must hurry home so she could give the egg to her mother. Perhaps they could have a very small omelet!

Anna took off the scarf she wore on her head. Carefully, she wrapped the egg in it and laid it tenderly in the basket with the beets. Then she got on her bicycle and started up the road.

But an unhappy thought came to her. The egg wasn't really hers. It belonged to the owner of the speckled hen. Anna's pedaling got slower and slower.

"No!" she told herself furiously, "the egg is mine. The hen laid it right beside me when I was asleep." Anna went on up the road. "Anyway, I don't know who owns the speckled hen. And even if I did, they would never know that I had the egg."

A little white house sat close to the road. "They can't tell a thing," argued Anna with herself. "I've got the egg all covered up." She began to pedal faster.

But her bicycle seemed to go more and more slowly. And when she got near the white house, her legs wouldn't pedal any longer. Very slowly, she got off her bicycle and walked up to the house.

"Yes?" asked the young woman who came to the door.

Very reluctantly, with her dream of the small omelet fading fast, Anna said, "Do . . . do . . . you own a . . . a . . . speckled hen?"

"Why yes," said the young woman, "we do." Carefully and very slowly, Anna unwrapped her scarf from around the egg and handed it to the woman.

"Then this is yours, too," she said in a small voice.

"Oh, thank you," said the woman. "That speckled hen is always wandering off and laying her eggs in the most unlikely places. She is the last of our hens, and we need her eggs for our little boy. He is very sick, you see."

Anna started to leave. The young woman looked troubled. "You have been so kind," she said. "I wish I had something to give you for your basket. But there is so little of everything. I . . . I . . . have nothing to give."

"It's all right," said Anna, and she climbed on her bicycle again. She was anxious now to get away from the little white house and the speckled hen and the wonderful egg.

When she got home, Anna told her mother what had happened. She was afraid her mother would scold her for being late, and for bringing home only a few beets. She might even be cross that Anna hadn't kept the egg.

But her mother only smoothed Anna's hair and looked at her for a long time, and smiled.

"Then you are not angry with me, Mother? You do not think I am too young to go to the country to bargain for vegetables?"

"No, Anna," said her mother, "I am just thinking what a fine daughter I have. When one is so hungry all the time, only a real grown-up could have made such a hard decision about the egg."

THE HOUSE THAT LOVE BUILT

By William W. Price

Setting: This is a true story. It happened in France after World War I where a whole village had been destroyed by the fighting.

Marie woke with a start to inky blackness and the familiar smell of dirt. Her small body shivered from the damp cold. As she roused herself to rearrange her rough bed of rags and burlap on the dirt floor, the nightmare that had jolted her from sleep closed around her head like a dark cloud. She had been having that nightmare every night.

It always started with a pleasant dream. She saw her beloved little French village. Then she could feel herself walking out of her old, cozy home with Maman and Grandmère and passing through the narrow street. Bright flowers were waving from boxes under nearly every window. The sun gleamed on the tall church steeple. But there was another, frightening gleam creeping toward their village—the gleam of guns. Marie shivered again as the happy dream turned to the dreaded nightmare. Black memories rolled through her head. Terrified, Maman and Grandmère had pulled her into the trees. There, the three of them had flattened themselves against the leafy ground. Blue uniformed soldiers passed in waves. Guns! Fight-

Adapted by the Committee. Used by permission of the author.

ing! Explosions and screams! Fire! When it was over, the village was not there any more.

When the battle had moved on, Marie and her mother and grandmother had tearfully sorted through the rubble that had been their home. The little family had moved into an old fruit cellar—"like gophers in a hole in the ground," Marie thought sadly.

She burrowed into her rags and fell back into a fitful sleep. The soldiers marched on and on through her head. After the French soldiers in blue uniforms had come the German soldiers in green ones. To everyone's relief, they soon left. Then had come the khaki uniforms of the Americans. The Americans had laughed and handed out French pennies to eager children. But when they left, the village was still in ruins.

When Marie woke again, sunlight was shining through the cracks between the old boards placed across the top of the fruit cellar as a roof. Hearing new sounds, she sat up quickly. This morning something different was happening. She wondered what the sounds could be.

"Maman, have the soldiers come back?" she asked anxiously.

"No, my dear. Go up and see who has arrived." Maman looked strangely pleased.

Marie threw off the ragged covers and climbed the rickety fruit-cellar steps. She saw immediately that new men in gray uniforms had come to the village. On their sleeves and on their caps, they wore a red and black star.

"Oh, Maman!" cried Marie excitedly after watching them for several minutes. "The star soldiers carry saws and hammers, not guns. They are building houses!"

Marie thought they were soldiers because they wore uniforms. But they were not soldiers. They were workers from the British and American Quaker Service Committees—perhaps the grandparents or great-grandparents of some of the children who are reading this story.

Marie thought quickly. She ran back down the old steps and grabbed an old sock. In it were six French pennies the

American soldiers had given her. It was the only money that anyone in the family had. As she hurried back up, anxious hope trembled in every step. She ran over to the leader of the men in gray.

Timidly, the small girl held out her tiny sock and showed the man her six pennies. "M'sieu, pouvez-vous me construire une maison pour six sous?" (Sir, can you build me a house for six cents?)

The man looked surprised and asked her to repeat her question. When he finally understood, he didn't laugh or even smile but replied quite seriously, "Well, Mademoiselle, we'll see what we can do."

He didn't say "Yes," but he didn't say "No" either. Marie set up a daily watch to see what would happen. One by one, small houses were finished for other people. Each house was small and simple, but to Marie, they looked beautiful. How she longed for clean wooden floors to sweep and a beautiful red tile roof to keep out the rain.

Would they leave before they built a house for her family? While she waited and watched, the fruit cellar seemed even darker and damper than ever.

Just when she was beginning to give up hope, Marie received her answer. The answer was "Yes!" Marie's house, like the others, was built in just three days. To Marie, it looked like the most beautiful house in the world.

On the day it was finished, the leader of the men in gray offered the front door key to Marie with great ceremony, saying, "Mademoiselle, le clef." (Miss, the key)

Marie took it and started to open the door officially, while her mother and grandmother and all the rest of the village looked on.

But suddenly she stopped, remembering something. She had offered them her six pennies for a house, so it wasn't really hers yet.

Quickly she ran down the old steps into the cellar and when she came up again, she walked up to the leader of the men in gray. Now that it was finished, the house looked big and six pennies began to look very small. But it was all she had, and she counted them out into the leader's hand. Un, deux, trois, quatre, cinq, six.

Would it be enough? She hardly dared look at the man's face.

The man smiled at her and said solemnly (in French, of course), "Thank you, Mademoiselle, but four pennies is quite enough." And he handed back two of her pennies.

Perhaps you wonder how Marie could buy a house for four pennies. It was because the French government supplied all the materials and the Quakers brought the tools and gave all the hours of work so people who had lost so much could have homes again to start a new life.

For information about ways the American Friends Service Committee is helping victims of violence today, write to them at 1501 Cherry Street, Philadelphia, PA 19102.

$$\equiv$$

A DUST RAG FOR EASTER EGGS

$$\equiv$$

By Claire Huchet Bishop

Setting: In France after World War II, food was scarce and almost everything else was too. Life was hard and many children had to take on adult responsibilities.

One afternoon after school, soon after the end of World War II, a group of five children were talking things over on a street corner in Paris. The name of the street was "rue du Chat qui Pêche"—The Street of the Cat Who Goes Fishing—and the children called themselves "The Gang of the Cat Who Goes Fishing."

Ten-year-old Charles was telling his friends about how weak his little sister Zézette was and what the doctor had said.

"He said," explained Charles, "that it is all because she has not had proper food. Not in the whole five years since she was born."

"It's tough," said twelve-year-old Louise, "with your father a prisoner in Germany and then dying a year after he came back. And poor Zézette not even knowing him."

Adapted by the Committee from "A Dust Rag for Easter Eggs," by Claire Huchet Bishop, *Child Life*, April, 1947, Open Road Publishing Company. Used by permission of the author.

"No use talking about that," said nine-year-old Jules. "It's what we do for Zézette now that counts."

"I wish we could give her a beautiful Easter," said Rémi.

"If only we could give her a chocolate Easter egg," said Louise.

"A chocolate egg!" said Paul, who was eight. "If only we could get just plain eggs!"

There was silence. After a while, Jules remarked, "There are plain eggs. In the country. If one can go there."

"Yes," agreed Charles. "That's what the doctor said. But he said you can't buy eggs in the country with money. You have to have things to exchange."

"But to barter from country people," Jules went on, "you have to have the real thing to offer, like shoes, a wool blanket, a sweater. . . ."

"Sure," said Rémi, "and nobody has any of those things any more."

"Except very rich people," said Paul.

"Come on," said Jules, "there's no use talking. Let's go to the Luxembourg Gardens."

"Good-bye," said Charles. "I have to get home. It's only 4:30 and Mother doesn't come back from work till 7 o'clock. I have to keep Zézette company."

The others said good-bye to Charles a little sadly and went on their way.

"Say," cried Jules, stopping the others. "Our gang ought to be able to do something about Zézette."

"Sure," agreed Paul, who was very fond of her. "Zézette belongs to the gang too."

Rémi turned to Louise. "You are so good at knitting, Louise. Couldn't you knit something and we could sell it—that is, barter it for eggs?"

"Knit with what?" asked Louise, her eyes blazing. "There isn't any yarn anywhere," she added bitterly.

They walked on in silence.

No, there was no yarn to be had anywhere. What could the gang find to barter for eggs? And Easter was only a month off.

"What? What?" thought Louise, lying awake that night. She and Rémi lived alone with their father. Louise was the woman of the family now, just as Charles was the man of the family in his house.

The next day was Thursday. It was house-cleaning day for Louise. She washed, she swept, she ran the dust rag over the furniture, she picked up the old wool rag to shake it out the window . . . and nearly dropped it in the street. The old, dirty rag was a discarded wool sweater of her mother's, so worn out and full of holes that Louise had never noticed it before, not really.

Carefully Louise spread the rag on the floor. "No," she thought, "it's hopeless. Even if I could wash it, it could not possibly be of any use." She sat there on the floor, fingering the dirty old rag.

Suddenly, she picked up the piece, shook it out the window a long time, then brushed it and set it to soak in a pan of water. She could not spare any soap. On Saturday night, instead of using soap for her own bath, she used it on the rag. And the next day she rinsed and rinsed until the water came all clear. Three days later the old wool rag was dry. It looked awful, but it was pretty clean.

Then Louise started to unravel the whole thing. It took her ages because it was all in pieces and she had to keep tying the pieces together. But finally she had four big balls of yarn. The next day, when they said good-bye to Charles after school, she showed the yarn to the rest of the gang. They touched it respectfully, and weighed it in their cupped hands.

"I'm going to make a sweater," Louise said.

"Won't be a pretty color," remarked Paul.

"What of it?" challenged Rémi somewhat angrily.

"He is right," said Louise. "It should be dyed. But I have no dye."

That evening, as Louise was getting supper, there was a knock at the door. It was Jules. He gave her an envelope. "Here is some dye," he said. "I stood in line two hours to get matches for the woman who runs the notions store, and in exchange she gave me the dye. Dark blue. That's all she had. So long! All for the gang!" he shouted, tumbling downstairs.

The yarn was dyed and Louise began to knit.

She was a fast knitter, and it was not long before she was working on the last sleeve. It was Thursday afternoon and she brought her work with her to show to the others.

The gang was very excited. Rémi was proud of his sister, and they started discussing how many eggs they might get for the sweater. Jules said sharply, "No use kidding ourselves. We won't get much. The wool is too thin in too many places."

"Louise, could you fill these thin places?" Rémi suggested. "Like embroidering something?"

"With what?" Louise asked bitterly. "There won't be any yarn left."

Paul jumped to his feet. "I know!" he shouted. "Mother has a bag of tiny pieces of yarn. All colors. She never throws anything away."

"Wonderful," said Louise, brightening up. "I could embroider all the thin spots with colored yarn."

That evening Paul set the table, wiped the dishes, took the garbage downstairs, all without being asked, and to top it all he went to bed without being told twice. When his mother came to say goodnight, she asked, "What's on your mind?" And Paul threw his arms around her and said, "How did you know?" Then he asked her if he could have some of her little pieces of colored yarn. His mother said, "Those pieces of yarn are very precious nowadays, Paul. You cannot have them to play with."

"I know," said Paul. "But it's for our gang. We are making something—something to trade for a present for Zézette be-cause she's sick."

"So," replied his mother, smiling, "you are trying to barter setting the table, wiping the dishes, taking the garbage down, and going to bed at once for my little pieces of colored yarn."

His mother stroked Paul's hair gently. "Zézette is a nice girl, isn't she? The gang is doing a good thing. You may have the pieces, a little at a time every day as long as needed, provided that during that time you keep helping me. Is that a bargain?"

"Check," said Paul, as he leaned back sleepily on his pillow.

And now it was Holy Week and the sweater was finished. It was all dotted here and there with bright-colored flowers and birds. It was beautiful. Rémi was chosen by the gang to go to the country and barter it for eggs. Rémi was a scout and had a bicycle.

Now it was the afternoon of Thursday before Easter, and Rémi was standing by his bicycle, ready to start. His father was saying, "Rather strange, this outing. Where will you sleep tonight, Rémi?"

"At a farm, Papa."

"Look here," said his father, "no matter if you are a scout, I don't like your riding around alone on country roads at night. You are too young."

"Please, Papa, let him go," called Louise. "He will be all right. We are not like children before the War."

Rémi rode along the highway, his bike bumping continuously into the holes. He had gotten out of Paris easily. There was practically no traffic at all, and now he was alone in the midst of the Montmorency forest. Trees, trees, trees. No houses. No cars except for an occasional jeep. The sun disappeared before Rémi was out of the forest. By ten o'clock he decided he had better try to sleep somewhere. It was too damp to sleep in the open. Fifty feet or so from the road he saw a faint light. He turned on a side lane and went toward the light. He nearly broke his lantern, bumping suddenly into a pile of rubble. The farm had been bombed.

Rémi knocked at the heavy door. A man's voice asked gruffly, "Who is there?"

"I am looking for a place to sleep, please," shouted Rémi.

The door was opened a crack and a storm-lantern flashed in Rémi's face.

"A boy!" said the man. "Come in."

Rémi went into the room crowded with all the stuff that had been saved from the bombing. He said, "Bonsoir, M'sieur, Madame."

"Bonsoir," said the man. "Leave your bike there against the wall. You can sleep on the bench if you want to. There is nothing else."

The woman went to the cupboard, took out a piece of dark bread and a pitcher of milk, and set them on the table.

"Sit down and eat. Eat as much as you want."

"But I have no money," said Rémi.

"Eat," ordered the man. "The wife told you."

Rémi came toward the table. "My name is Rémi Renault," he said.

"Ours, it's Bonnet." They shook hands and the three of them sat down. Rémi was very hungry. He ate the whole hunk of dark bread and drank the whole pitcher of milk. The man asked how things were in Paris . . . if there was enough food.

"We were bombed. We have just one cow left and a few chickens . . . and," he whispered, "our sorrow."

"Have you a little sister?" asked the woman abruptly of Rémi.

"No," said Rémi, "but there is Zézette. It's because of her that I am here."

And he told them the whole story. Zézette's sickness. The doctor's advice. The gang. The dust rag. The dye. The colored pieces of yarn. The sweater, and their wish for real eggs.

They listened quietly with a funny little expression in their eyes, as if they were about to weep.

"Let us see the sweater," they said. Rémi showed it to them.

"Never seen anything prettier," said the woman. "And to think that it all came out of a dirty old dust rag!"

"If you go a little farther north tomorrow morning," said the man, "there they have not been bombed and you should be able to get a lot of food in exchange for this sweater." Rémi's eyes sparkled.

"You're a good child," said Madame Bonnet. "I dare say all of your gang are good children . . . like my little angel who is in heaven," she added softly.

When Rémi woke the next morning, he saw there was milk again on the table and another piece of dark bread. The sweater was spread out and next to it were a dozen eggs.

"Bonjour," greeted Madame Bonnet. "Come and eat before you go."

"Here are a dozen eggs for Zézette," said Monsieur Bonnet.

"So you do like the sweater!" cried Rémi.

"My boy, the sweater is worth much more than that. We cannot afford to bargain for that sweater. But we want you to take the eggs for Zézette."

"But," said Rémi, "what can I give . . . I don't understand."

"The eggs, we give them to you." And seeing Rémi's puzzled expression, Monsieur Bonnet added, "Sort of like to be honorary members of the gang."

"Listen, Rémi," broke in Madame Bonnet gently, "we had a Zézette too. Only her name was Clotilde. She would be five years old now. She was killed in the air raid."

Rémi said quietly, "Ah, poor Monsieur and Madame Bonnet."

They stood silent.

"I guess I'd better be going," said Rémi. He arranged the eggs, carefully wrapped, in the wire basket on his bike.

Monsieur Bonnet said, "Turn left on the main road and go as far as the big crossroad where the shrine is. Then turn right there and you will see a big, prosperous farm. They have not been bombed out. You can barter the sweater, and be sure you get plenty for it."

He squared his shoulders and said, "Look here, Rémi, I have not asked my wife, but I would like to let you have more eggs in two or three weeks, if you can manage to come back."

"Do what my husband says, Rémi," said Madame Bonnet.

"I'll come back! I'll manage it!" He shook hands with them. He swung onto his bike, turned around and shouted, "And may the good God bless you and send you another child."

Rémi found the way just as Monsieur Bonnet had told him. And at the prosperous farm he bartered the sweater and got for it:

- ❖ three pounds of new potatoes
- ❖ a mess of salad greens
- ❖ a pound of butter
- ❖ a jar of honey

—*and* a big fat chicken!

Rémi had a hard time getting back to Paris. The basket was heavy and he was holding the bag of potatoes in his left hand so that he had only his right hand to steer the bike and steady himself over the bumps. He reached home after sundown on Good Friday, just as his father was coming in. And then, of course, everything had to be explained. Papa looked upset at first, and then very happy. He said, "I'm proud of you and Louise!"

"But Papa," said Louise, "it is not Rémi and I only. It's the gang. I made the sweater from the dust rag. Jules got the dye, Paul the colored pieces of yarn, and Rémi bartered the sweater."

"And what did Charles do?" asked Papa.

"He took care of Zézette," said Louise.

"Yes, he did," said Rémi. "He stayed with her every afternoon. That was the hardest of all."

"Well, well, well," mused Papa. "And now there is all this food. . . . How about having the whole gang here to eat it on Easter Sunday?"

So they did. The whole gang came: Louise, Rémi, Jules, Paul, Charles, and Zézette, who got up especially for the feast. What an Easter it was! How they ate! Zézette was presented with the eggs from the Bonnets and Rémi had to tell over and over again, "They said so. I can go back and get some more."

It was a beautiful Easter that year!

And now another Easter is coming. Louise, Rémi, Jules, Paul, Charles, and Zézette, who is well now, are all sitting in the Luxembourg Gardens, looking at a letter that Rémi has received. It is addressed to The Gang of the Cat Who Goes Fishing. It says:

Monsieur and Madame Bonnet
have the joy of announcing
the birth of their daughter
Clotilde-Zézette-Charlotte-Louise-
Mimi-Julia-Paulette Bonnet

WE KNOW THAT MAN

By Amelia Swayne and Hanna Still

There once lived in England a young doctor who had thought and read much about Africa. He was interested in the people who were there and wanted to be friends with them. Perhaps he might be able to teach them; certainly he could learn much from them if he could live and work with them for a time. Finally the opportunity came. He was chosen to go as a missionary to a small, remote village.

He set out with great joy. When he arrived at the village, he found many people to welcome him. He simply introduced himself as "Doctor Dave" and set to work. There was much work to be done: getting to know everybody, learning the language they spoke, visiting sick people, preparing lessons for those who wanted to learn to read. His aid was sought on problems as they arose. He took time to tell stories to the children, to play games with them, and to learn the songs they liked to sing.

Every night Dave was supposed to write down the work he had done during that day. Once a month he was to send what he had written to the people in England who had sent him.

The day the moon became full was the day the mail boat made its stop on its long trek upstream. It was a good three-

Adapted from a story told by Elfrida Vipont Foulds and Henry Hodgkin.

hour hike from his home to the river, so that day he would get up very early, put his notes into a big envelope, and set out in plenty of time.

Cheers went up every month as the boat landed. The captain would distribute the mail he had brought to eagerly waiting hands. Without fail, each month, there was a letter with money for Dave from his home office in England. Then the captain would reach for his large mail pouch. Anyone who wished to mail a letter would stuff it into the pouch. Every month Dave mailed off his big fat envelope with reports to the people back in England at the home office.

One day, as Dave was on his way to the river, he saw a man sitting alone, under a tree, weeping bitterly. Dave sat down by the man quietly. The weeping man knew Dave was sharing his sadness. He began to tell this tale: "My heart is heavy, my heart is so sad. I have done evil. I do not know what to do. The people of my village sent me to another village with money to buy sheep. Instead, I used the money for myself. When I returned to my village, I told them that I lay down to rest and someone took the money while I slept. I cannot return the money because I no longer have it. I cannot tell them what really happened. Not only I, but my whole family would be in disgrace. I must think of my children. I am so sick at heart. What am I to do?"

They sat and talked for many hours. Finally Dave suggested that he would talk to the captain of the mail boat. Possibly he might have heard of someone who needed a good worker. The man promised to work harder than he had ever worked in his life. When he had earned as much money as he had stolen, he would return to his village and beg for their forgiveness. Dave knew he had missed the river boat by this time. No use continuing his journey. Instead, he returned home, glad in his heart that he had encountered the sad man and shared his sorrow, and might be able to help him.

The following month, Dave set out as usual to meet the river boat. His mind was so occupied with making a wish list to his home office for more medical supplies that he was unaware of a group of men running to meet him until they were almost upon him. A very small child had been bitten by a poisonous snake. The three men were taking turns carrying the little child in search of help.

Instantly, Dave went to work. First he needed to clean his knife. He could clean his knife if he could make a fire and boil some water. He told the men to gather a little pile of dead sticks. Then he set to work letting the sun shine through a little magnifying glass upon the only paper he had with him—part of his report to the home office in England.

A little smoke appeared, then a tiny spark. With the burning paper, he lit the pile of little sticks and heated water in his drinking cup. Then he cleaned his knife in the boiling water. With the clean knife, he was able to help the child. He assured the men that he would come to see the child that evening and continued on his way to the river.

Alas! When he arrived at the shore, he saw the mail boat disappearing upstream, well beyond shouting distance.

The month after, Dave rose early and headed for the river boat. About half way, as the path made a sharp turn, Dave surprised two men quarreling fiercely. It seemed to him that the bigger was about to hit the smaller one, but stopped when he saw Dave. "If I go on," thought Dave, "this fight will continue the minute I am out of sight. I'd best stop."

It turned out that the two young men were brothers. The elder felt that his father made him work much harder than his brother. "You will always have anger between you," observed Dave, "but you cannot settle this quarrel between yourselves. Your father needs to be part of the only peace that will last. Let me go home with you and see if we can all talk together."

Dave spoke very politely to the father. More than anything, the father wanted peace in the family. He agreed to divide the work fairly and the young men agreed not to quarrel any more.

Since Dave knew that he had missed the river boat again, he ate with the family and spent the night there. Early the next morning, he set out for his home, treasuring the new friendships he had made.

The next month, Dave decided to set out for the river the day before the boat was due to arrive. He camped that night at the river bank. As the sun rose in the sky, the boat became visible. Relief filled Dave's heart. Soon he would talk to the captain. He would receive much mail. He would send off his fatter-than-ever envelope to his home office, including explanations of why he had not succeeded in mailing off the earlier reports on time.

Dave saw surprise on the captain's face. "Since I have not seen you for months, I assumed you had left these parts, and I returned the mail that had accumulated for you. I have only one letter for you today," he said.

Dave opened the letter in haste. It read,

We have just received the mail we have been sending you, returned to us. We have received no reports from you for three months.

It is evident that you have failed to represent our Board of Missions in Africa. We have had to assume that you are no longer interested. We hereby declare our association to be finished, and request that you immediately move out of the quarters we provided for you.

Dejected by his failure, in dismay about his future, embarrassed by the tears in his eyes, Dave let his fat envelope slip out of his hands and fall into the river. He waved good-bye to the captain and started slowly back through the woods.

Many years passed.

The office in England decided to send more workers to the part of Africa where Dave had been. One day two missionaries arrived at a small forest clearing. They had paddled many miles up the river. The Africans gathered around them, welcomed them, and asked why they had come.

The missionaries said, "We have come to teach you about a great and good man. He went around the country helping people. He healed those who were sick. He taught many valuable lessons through stories. He loved children and had a special way with them."

As they spoke, their listeners smiled and nodded to each other and became more and more pleased. When the missionaries stopped for breath, the people said, "Oh yes, we know that man. We know him well."

"No," said the missionaries gently. "He lived about 2000 years ago in Palestine, a country far from here. You could not know him."

"But we do," was the reply. "Come, we will take you to him."

Much puzzled, the missionaries followed the people as they walked happily along a well-worn path to a small hut. Beside it sat a man telling a story to a group of children. He smiled and rose to greet his neighbors as they approached.

The missionaries stared in amazement. Here was Doctor Dave, who had been asked to leave the mission so many years before!

MARTIN DE PORRES PLANTS AN ORCHARD

By Claire Huchet Bishop

Setting: In Lima, Peru, after the Spanish conquest, the Spanish masters enjoyed great wealth, while the native Inca Indians and black people lived in terrible poverty. This story is about a Dominican monk, half Spanish and half black, who lived at that time.

As a boy, Martin de Porres knew how it felt not to have enough to eat and to suffer because of having one Spanish parent and one black one. But he harbored no bitterness, and when he grew up, he became a monk.

Part of his work was at a convent farm. Working in the fields did him good, and gradually his sadness would melt away. The country all around was covered with orchards, and because of the mildness of the climate and the excellent system of irrigation that the Spanish had learned from the Incas, the crops were good year after year.

One day as he was walking along a country road on his way to the farm, he was passing a fig orchard when he heard the noise of cracking branches and saw spots of color up in a tree. He went toward it and discovered two ragged children hidden up in the tree.

"What are you doing up there?"

"Nothing," said the boy.

"We never have any figs at our house," said the girl.

"We can't afford them. They cost too much."

Martin knew what that meant. He remembered the pain and hunger of his own childhood.

"Come down," he ordered.

They did, looking very scared. In Lima, stealing from the orchards meant jail for children. Martin sat down by the roadside and motioned for them to sit, too, on either side of him. He was very quiet, for what seemed to the children a long time. They did not dare disturb him. His eyes were closed. Perhaps he was praying. When he opened them at last, he said quietly, "Would you like to have your own fig orchard, your very own, where you could go and eat freely whenever you wanted to?"

They looked at him with questioning eyes. He had not scolded them. He had said nothing about jail. Evidently he was all right. But to ask if they would like to have their own orchard! He must be a little out of his mind.

"You got loads of money?" inquired the boy cautiously. Martin shook his head.

"Then," said the boy, "about the orchard of our own, that's just a nice story, eh?"

Martin put his hands in the wide sleeves of his Monk's robe and brought out two figs. "Oh!" they shrieked, "where did you get them?"

He laughed happily. "That's the beginning of the orchard," he said. "Now, no more stealing, understand? You come and see me at the convent farm, Limatombo, the day after tomorrow."

"Why?"

"About your orchard."

As soon as Martin arrived at the farm, he paid a visit to the horses and the mules. With incredible speed he washed and brushed them, put clean hay in their stables, and brought them feed, all the while talking to them.

Whenever Martin came to the farm, it was like a holiday for the animals. They always welcomed him noisily, whinnying, stamping their feet, and flinging their tails. Taking care of them was an extra chore that Martin voluntarily took upon himself.

That day, he was supposed to plant some new fig trees. As soon as he was through with the animals, he set to work, carefully preparing the soil and handling each sapling with respect and love, offering it to God and the Blessed Virgin before planting it in the ground. He seemed to go at it slowly, but it was only because his gestures were rhythmical, like a dance. As a matter of fact, he was working very fast, because he wanted to have some extra time left.

While he was at the farm he inquired if there was any piece of land that did not yet belong to anybody. There was! He went to see it. When he came back the next day he worked faster than ever, and on the third day, in the morning, he finished with the planting he was supposed to do. There were some saplings left over, so he set them aside, and just as he did so the two children arrived.

They were not alone. They had brought with them several of their friends, other poor children of the Lima slums. Pointing to them the two children said to Martin, "They want an orchard, too."

"Fine! Fine!" exclaimed Martin. "That's the spirit. Now, you girls, take all the saplings. And you boys, here are spades. And now, let's go."

"Where to?" they inquired.

"To your orchard!"

Ah! What a day of happiness this was! Martin and the boys and girls planted the little trees on the unclaimed piece of land. Their orchard, the orchard of the poor children in Lima, for years to come!

Many such an orchard did Martin plant in his lifetime: fig, olive, and orange, which became the common property of the poor people of Lima. Martin showed the people, children and adults, how to cultivate and harvest. In this way, many children whose parents could not afford a private orchard had plenty of fruit.

Although the original trees have had to be replaced, the orchards, after four hundred years, are still there—a continuing gift of love.

THE HELP THAT STRETCHED FROM THEN TO NOW

By Carol Passmore and Janet Sabina

Back in 1937, when your grandparents or maybe even your great-grandparents were the age you are now, a young farmer in Indiana named Dan West heard about a far-away war. It was happening across the ocean, in Spain. Dan decided to go there and help.

You might think he was going to help fight. No. He was from the Church of the Brethren, one of the peace churches. He went because he wanted to help people who were suffering because of the war. Many had been driven away from their homes by the fighting and didn't have enough to eat.

Quakers in the American Friends Service Committee had started a project to help these people and were glad to have Dan's help.

Dan's first job was to stir water into powdered milk and put it in tin cups for children to drink. He watched the thin children in ragged clothes pick up the cups and gulp the milk eagerly. They looked at him with sad, frightened eyes.

Dan felt sad, too, terribly sad. He was glad to be giving them food, but he knew that even when the war was over, it would be a long time before their families would be able to get milk for them. What would happen when he left?

Dan felt helpless. So much needed to be done, and he was just one person.

Then he had an idea. A cow could make milk every day. Why not send cows instead of just powdered milk?

Dan West went home with this idea. He told everyone who would listen to him. It took five years, but finally a ship sailed across the ocean with eighteen young heifer cows on it. Soon there would be twice as many cows because all the heifers were pregnant.

A special rule had been added to Dan West's idea. Anyone who was given a pregnant cow had to promise to give away the first calf to another hungry family. That way, two families would be helped by each gift. Besides, being given something can make a person feel small. Being able to give something away can make a person feel generous and big.

The experiment with that first load of heifers worked so well that soon more loads of pregnant animals were being sent to other places where people were hungry and feeling helpless and discouraged. Heifer Project International was organized to get the animals and send them where they were needed.

Heifer Project International is still sending heifers, but today they go by airplane instead of by ship. Loads of pigs, goats, sheep, chickens, ducks, rabbits, camels, yaks, even bees are also being sent. In fact, in Senegal, West Africa, the peanut crop had gotten very poor because pesticides and a drought had killed off the bees that usually pollinated the peanut plants. A load of bees solved that problem, besides providing honey for the people to eat or sell. These days, Heifer Project International also sends people to teach the new owners how to take care of their animals. It sends medicine for animals too. It pays for the animals and the boats, the teachers and the medicines, with money contributed by people like you. Its motto is "Good Neighbor to the World."

In Honduras today, across the ocean from Spain, there is a little girl named Esolina Marinez who was dying because she had never had enough good food to make her healthy. Esolina's father was given a pregnant goat. Goats give about five cups of milk a day, and that was enough to save Esolinia's life. When their goat had a kid, Esolinia's father followed the rule. He gave the kid to another family.

Later, the goat had more kids, who grew up to give more milk. Now Esolina's family have more milk than they need to drink. So they make cheese to sell. That gives them money to buy other things they need.

A man who delivered a heifer to a family in Germany wrote, "That evening a knock came at our door and the woman to whom we had given the cow stood before me. She said simply, 'I forgot to thank you.' I replied, 'You thanked me for the cow. But,' she said, 'I didn't thank you for the love. It takes a lot of love to give a cow.'"

Dan West's idea has stretched across years and countries. It is over fifty years old now, and families in more than a hundred countries and many of our states have been given a chance to help themselves and their neighbors in this way. It shows how one person can make a difference.

If you want to know more about Heifer Project International, write to them at P.O. Box 808, Little Rock, Arkansas 72203 or call 1-800-422-0474.

TO SAN LUIS, WITH LOVE

By Gordon Browne

When she graduated from college in 1977, Ann Kriebel, a birthright Quaker, was not sure what she wanted to do with her life. She had enjoyed studying Spanish, and she had met some Friends from the Quaker community at Monteverde in Costa Rica. She went there.

Monteverde is a dairy farming community with a cooperative cheese-making plant. Life was simple and good, but Ann did not find her niche there. She returned to the United States to teach English to Latin American refugees and immigrants in Boston. Then, after several years, she felt she finally knew what she wanted to do. She would go back to Monteverde to write children's books in Spanish.

Monteverde is on a wide shelf, high in the mountains that form the continental divide in Costa Rica. From the shelf of Monteverde, the mountain slope plunges precipitously to the San Luis River Valley below. Though public education has been part of Costa Rican life for more than eighty years, the San Luis Valley is so remote that many adults there had never learned to read or write when Ann arrived. For low wages they worked hard on other people's land and owned none of their own. The Valley was a stagnant backwater of Costa Rican life.

A young man from San Luis named Eugenio Vargas had left the Valley and gone to college. He was concerned about the plight of the people at home, however, and he and his wife had returned to San Luis to live and to work. He had dreams of stirring that backwater.

Somehow, he and Ann met. Eugenio took Ann down into the Valley to meet its people. She was touched by their friendliness, their simplicity and dignity, their courage. But she was dismayed by their passive acceptance of the limitations on their lives. What would help them? Eugenio said they needed to learn to read and write if they were to have the resources to change their lives.

Ann said, "I have done some teaching. Could I help?"

Excitedly, the two began to talk of an adult literacy program for San Luis Valley. They went to the people of the Valley. Would they like to learn to read and write?

The people were cautious. "There are no books or papers here. We have no supplies," they said warily.

"We'll make our own books!" Ann said. "You can tell me the stories of your lives, of the life in the Valley. I will write it all down, and we will learn to read it."

It had never occurred to these humble, hard-working people that their lives were worthy of such telling, of such attention. But Ann's idea pleased them. They would like to try.

"We will need supplies, though," Eugenio cautioned. "We'll need paper and pencils and some books."

"Yes, and paints and crayons, too!" Ann said, her vision expanding. "The Right Sharing of World Resources Program supports projects like this. It's a program of Friends World Committee for Consultation. I'll write and ask for what we'll need."

So Ann wrote to the Committee in Philadelphia, asking for $4000 to pay for an adult literacy project in the San Luis Valley. Some of the money would cover her own expenses, permitting her to work on the project full time.

Ann did not wait for a response. She began immediately organizing classes: for the young mothers, for the older women, for the working men, for the older men. Each day she walked down from Monteverde to the Valley, carrying her own paper and pencils. The San Luisanos thought about their lives and told their stories while she wrote them down. Then, together, they would look at what she had written and connect the pencil marks with what the people had said. Each day at dusk, she climbed back up the long trail to Monteverde.

The trail from Monteverde down into San Luis is rocky and steep. A strong walker can make it in an hour and a half, a horse with rider in a little less time. Worried about Ann's ability to maintain so strenuous a schedule, Eugenio got her a horse. After that, she rode down to the Valley each morning and rode back up at evening.

One day going down, she felt the cinch on her saddle let go. The saddle slipped to one side, and she was thrown hard on the rocky trail. Bruised and bleeding, she fixed the cinch, remounted, and went on to the Valley to teach all day, before returning to Monteverde for medical attention.

In November of 1982, several months after she had sent her request, the Right Sharing Committee approved Ann's application for $4000. With funds at last available, the San Luis Valley project "took off." A women's group had formed in the Valley and was discussing nutrition and preventive medicine. Some of the young people wanted to learn first aid. The men were struggling to keep up with their classes and still work enough hours to earn the money they needed to feed their families. A community council had been formed to plan community events and improvements. The people themselves, with Eugenio's help, were deciding what they needed to do. Ann was providing the skills and the spirit.

For Ann was a talented musician. She played the guitar and wrote many songs of her own. She soon had the San Luisanos, as part of their writing lessons, writing poems about their Valley. Ann set the words to music, and they all sang them. She and Eugenio persuaded the government to give the community some books to start a library. The local Catholic priest provided more. So did the Friends in Monteverde, who were caught up in Ann's enthusiasm for the project, in her love for the San Luisanos, and in her excitement as she watched her friends take charge of their own lives.

The finest poet and musician in the Valley was a young man with a withered right leg which did not reach even to the bottom of his pants leg. Despite his bad leg, he became a leader in the community council and a lay teacher in the catechism classes in the Catholic Church. Describing what Ann meant to him and to others in the Valley, he said, "I was born crippled. I was so ashamed of my leg that I would not leave the house. I spoke with no one but my family. I lived entirely in my imagination. That's where my poems and songs came from.

"Then Ann came." He paused, looking for just the right words. "She met me. She accepted me. She loved me. She freed me."

The big issue for the community council was land. The workers yearned to start a cooperative farm. But more than half the land in the San Luis Valley was owned by one absentee landlord, who would sell none of it. A Friend in Monteverde told Eugenio about Vinoba Bhave, one of Gandhi's followers in India, who had walked all over the country, asking rich people for gifts of land to distribute to the poor. Why couldn't Eugenio do that in San Luis?

Excited by the idea, Eugenio went to the other land owners of the Valley, asking them to give land for the poor workers. Two of them did—some 250 acres! Twenty-two families joined together to form the cooperative farm.

The literacy classes were producing beautiful poems and stories about the traditions of the people of the San Luis Valley. The women's group was talking about women's rights and women's responsibilities in Latin American society. The men were clearing land for the cooperative farm. And always the people sang—Ann's songs, their songs, funny songs, game songs, songs of love for their Valley and their homes.

Then Ann got sick, some kind of cold, a fever. She went to bed for several days, missing her classes for the first time. The fever got worse. Against her wishes, Ann was carried down the mountain from Monteverde to a hospital in the city of San José, where modern medical care would be available. Although they gave her all sorts of tests, the doctors could not diagnose her disease. Ten days after she had fallen ill, Ann died, at the age of 28.

Friends in Monteverde were stunned. That such a beautiful young life should be taken from them! They planned a Quaker memorial service, based on silent waiting upon God. They invited Eugenio and his wife and all the people of the San Luis Valley. Ann's parents came from Ohio.

On the day of the service, the entire San Luis community wound its way up the mountainside to Monteverde, some carrying wild flowers of the Valley that Ann had loved. And as the silence deepened in worship, they stood, one by one, and read—these people who just a year before had been unable to read or to write—they read their poems of love to Ann. Some sang their songs. And they wept with their new friends in Monteverde.

Eugenio Vargas and the San Luis community continue to reshape the life of their Valley. Visits back and forth with Friends in Monteverde are frequent. The cooperative farm sends its milk to the Monteverde cheese factory. The literacy classes, the women's group, the nutrition classes go on. And the loving, joyful spirit of Ann Kriebel is in all they do.

ELIZABETH FRY

By Elinor Briggs

*"A light to the blind, speech to the dumb,
and feet to the lame"*

Setting: Born into a wealthy English family in 1780, Elizabeth Fry could
have had a lifetime of ease. But she felt called to do something quite different.

When Elizabeth Gurney was a little girl, called Betsy by
her family, she enjoyed the pleasures of singing,
dancing, and parties in her family's beautiful home,
Earlham Hall. She also enjoyed reading many books in the
unusually large family library, but she was a frail, sickly child,
often with a headache or upset stomach. She never dreamed
that when she was sixteen years old, someone would look in
her eyes and tell her that she would be "a light to the blind,
speech to the dumb, and feet to the lame." Nor would she have
believed that she would give up the activities she enjoyed, as
well as her colorful dresses with laces and ruffles for the dull,
unadorned clothes and bonnet of the "plain" Quakers of the
1800s.

"I think I'll go to 'Goats' this morning," sixteen-year-old
Betsy Gurney told her sisters one First-Day morning. "Goats"
was their name for Goat's Lane Friends Meeting in Norwich,
where they were members.

"But Betsy, I thought you didn't feel well!" Her sisters couldn't believe that anyone would choose to go to the Friends' Meeting for the long, boring two hours of quiet when she didn't have to go.

"There is supposed to be a well-known Friend from America visiting today," Betsy explained. "Maybe something interesting will be said. I do think my headache is better. Besides, I think Uncle Joseph is beginning to think that I'm not getting to Meeting as often as I ought."

Uncle Joseph was a "plain" Friend who took very seriously his responsibility for the religious life of his brother's ten motherless children.

On this First-Day morning, the seven brightly dressed Gurney sisters hurried into the meetinghouse, late as usual. They took the only empty seats left, on the front row, facing the ministers' gallery. William Savery, the visiting Friend, was shocked! He had been speaking to crowds of people while traveling across England but was usually silent at the Friends' meetings he visited. But here, sitting directly in front of him, was Betsy, turning her foot this way and that, admiring her new purple boots with scarlet laces. He felt he must speak!

"Your fathers, where are they, and the prophets, do they live forever?"

These words, spoken in a clear and musical voice, got Betsy's attention. She felt hot all over. He was speaking to her! Was he calling her a "pretend" Quaker, one who was not living as the early Quakers had suffered prison and ridicule to be allowed to live? Her journal doesn't tell us what else he said, but these words she never forgot.

Thanks to the family custom of going home with Uncle Joseph for dinner following Meeting, Betsy had a chance to talk alone with William Savery. She began to feel sure that there was a God, a God who wanted her to become a true Friend.

Later that summer, visiting a cousin, Betsy met another influential Quaker, Deborah Darby. During a Meeting for Worship, Deborah looked straight at Betsy and told her, "You are to be a light to the blind, speech to the dumb, and feet to the lame." Betsy returned home filled with joy. That was what she wanted! Something worth while to do! When the family returned to Earlham Hall, she was impatient to start. She provided food to hungry families in a nearby village. She had always visited the sick and did so now with renewed energy. Was this being "feet to the lame"?

Her spelling was atrocious, and her writing was poor. She would work to improve them. She became aware that the poor children in the area had no chance to learn to read or write. Starting with one little boy, she quickly became the teacher for sixty. Her sisters called them "Betsy's imps." They came faithfully each First-Day afternoon. Was this being "a light to the blind"?

At this time, a "plain" Friend from London, Joseph Fry, came to court Betsy. But she was not ready to be married or to be a "plain" Friend. She sent him away very firmly. As time passed, however, and he returned again and again, she saw that he was, indeed, the one with whom she wished to spend the rest of her life.

Married life in the city of London, in a large, dark house called "Mildred's Court," was very different from her life in the beautiful, relaxed country home at Earlham Hall. The house was close to Grace Church Street Meeting, the center of the Religious Society of Friends at that time, and Friends had become used to making the Frys' home a place to stop and stay at any time. Suddenly, at eighteen years of age, Elizabeth Fry had to manage a large household and a constant stream of guests, sometimes as many as sixty for dinner!

She became a very good manager. Even with the eleven children that she and Joseph eventually had, she continued to tend the sick, feed the hungry, and work for better children's education.

After the sad time when her father died, Elizabeth found to her surprise that she had a gift in the ministry. Her voice was clear and musical. God gave her messages that people felt in their hearts. Was this being "speech to the dumb"? Feeling that it was very important, she traveled in the ministry, but it meant that she was away from home and her children more than some people thought was right.

Still, to Elizabeth, all these activities didn't seem to be what Deborah Darby had meant in that Meeting for Worship.

Meanwhile, people depended on her and kept calling on her for help. So Elizabeth was not surprised when a Friend from America, Stephen Grellet, knocked on the Frys' door one cold January day in 1813. Stephen was a young French nobleman who had fled to America during the French revolution and been befriended by Quakers there. He, too, had been influenced by Deborah Darby.

Traveling wherever he felt God called him, he had started visiting prisons. At first, it was to help the French soldiers who had been taken prisoner in America during the war with England. He found the prisons crowded with men suffering from cold, filth, cruel chains, and despair. Since they couldn't speak English, they couldn't even ask for what they needed. Stephen Grellet helped them.

When he came to London, he obtained a permit to visit Newgate Prison. While there, he passed the women's part and was horrified at what he saw. As soon as he left, he went directly to the Frys' house.

To Elizabeth, he described the women's infirmary this way: "I found many very sick, lying on bare floor or on some old straw, having very little scanty covering over them, though it was quite cold and there were several children born in prison among them almost naked." [1]

As soon as Stephen Grellet left, Elizabeth sent word to a group of her friends and got out some big pieces of flannel. Together, they worked late into the night, making clothes for the children.

The next morning, Elizabeth and her friend Anne Buxton climbed down from a carriage at the gates of the prison carrying many bundles of clothing and blankets. Grumbling and wondering why nice women would want to go into the infirmary, the jailors guided them past the women's courtyard. Many

---

[1] Benjamin Seebohm, *Memoirs of the Life of Stephen Grellet*, p. 224.

hands reached through the bars to grab at them, and screaming, whining voices begged them for a few pennies. But they continued on their way to the infirmary.

Despite the horror they felt at the sickness, filth, and smells, they set to work with kind words and gentle hands and paid the guards to bring them warm water and fresh straw. By the end of the day, the children were washed and clothed, and the women were lying on fresh straw, covered with warm blankets.

Two more times Elizabeth and Anne returned to care for the women, doing as much as they were permitted to do. The prayers they offered when they left the last day were received with grateful tears. Elizabeth knew that sometime she must return.

With all the demands on her time and energy, it was four years before Elizabeth was able to visit Newgate Prison again. Because of business troubles, the Frys had to sell their country home and do other things to save money. Elizabeth's family, the Gurneys, helped by paying the older boys' way at boarding school and taking the older girls into their own homes. Elizabeth, with only three children at home to care for, now had the time to return to the prison.

This time she had a plan. At fifteen she had gone with her father to visit a prison in Norwich. She had seen the filth and idleness, the crowding of sick and insane people with murderers and debtors, and knew of many other injustices in prisons. Now she was ready to try to improve such conditions at Newgate Prison.

The Governor of Newgate Prison wasn't sure he wanted to let this plainly dressed Quaker lady go into his prison. She might make trouble and even get into trouble herself. But Elizabeth was very persuasive, and finally he granted her a permit.

When she got to the gate, the guards warned, "You must not go in alone! They'll tear at your clothes! *We* dare not go in alone!"

Elizabeth insisted. She had a permit to enter the large room where the noisy, dirty women were shoving against the gate. And—she was going in alone!

The guards unlocked the gate. There was an astonished silence as Elizabeth walked quietly into the room in her plain Quaker dress with no ruffles, feathers, or shiny buttons to be grabbed. Smiling, she opened the Bible she was carrying, and in her clear, musical voice she read the story of the laborers who came late to work in the vineyard. Closing the Bible, she assured them that, as the story said, it was never too late to turn to God.

Then she reached down and picked up a filthy child. Holding the child, she told them that she had children too. Didn't the women want their children to have a better life than this? She was ready to help them. They were to choose a woman who could read to be a teacher. She would return to help them start a school for the children.

The women must have wondered whether to believe her. Many promises to them had been broken. But hope made them choose a woman to be ready to teach the children to read—if Elizabeth came back.

She did return when she said she would. A dirty, empty cell that could be used for the classroom was cleaned out by the women, and with her persuasive talent, she received permission from the Governor to use it.

"It won't work!" she was told by the jailors. "They won't be quiet or still for a minute!"

But they were. Those under twenty-five were allowed in the class. Some who were left out crowded around the door. It was true that others, who were not included, were as noisy and dirty as ever, running wildly around, snatching at everyone's clothes, swearing and gambling away what few pennies they had.

Elizabeth saw that more than that class was needed, and she could not do it all herself. She gathered together a group of women who called themselves "An Association for the Improvement of the Female Prisoners at Newgate." They started at once to work on a plan to make the conditions better for all the women.

They made a list of requests to take to the Governor. One was that women prisoners might have women jailors. The women needed clothes; why not teach them to sew and knit? This would keep them busy and quiet and make them better able to find work when they were released from prison.

Elizabeth and her friends approached the Governor and the other officers of the prison with their ideas, taking care not to offend them. At first, the men ridiculed their ideas and called the women dreamers. The prisoners would never sit down and work. At the least, they would tear the material into shreds. But finally, the women were given permission to try it. After all, the school was very successful.

Elizabeth started by making a list of twelve rules that the women must agree to obey. One was that they would be divided into groups of twelve, with the most orderly one as their leader, a "monitor." The monitor would be responsible for handing out the materials each day and collecting them later. Another rule was that they must come to work with clean hands and faces and be quiet while they worked. Elizabeth explained each of the rules, one at a time, giving the prisoners time to discuss them. She wanted them to feel that they had a part in the plan. When she had finished, they all agreed to follow them. The prison authorities spoke to the women too, giving the rules more power and authority.

Before long, the word spread that the terrible women's side of Newgate prison had become a clean and orderly place. It became fashionable to come and watch the women sew quietly or listen to Elizabeth Fry or another member of the Association read the Bible to them.

Rejoicing in the successes, Elizabeth must have thought, "Now I know how I am to be 'a light to the blind, speech for the dumb, and feet for the lame.'" But when she was praised for her work at Newgate, she reminded people that the good that was happening was God's doing, and that she was only God's tool.

A committee of Parliament invited her to come and tell about her experiences in Newgate Prison. Except for the Queen, only men were usually permitted to speak there. The men must have been surprised when Elizabeth spoke to them with her musical voice and calm manner. Her practice in speaking in Friends' meetings made it possible for her to think clearly and give good answers to their questions.

Despite the improvements at Newgate, Elizabeth saw other injustices. The authorities had two ways of dealing with the bad overcrowding in the prisons. One was to use the death penalty, even for stealing some small thing. The other was to send prisoners to the far-away colony in Australia. That meant a rough, two-month trip by ship, chained below decks with no sun, air, or anything to do, and arriving with no money or job, perhaps becoming slaves.

One day, Elizabeth arrived at the prison to find the place in an uproar. When she asked the jailors what was wrong, they explained that a group of women were to be sent to a prison ship tomorrow.

"We always have a bad night before they go," said a jailor. "They get drunk, tear things up, set fires, and fight everyone. Then in the morning, we have to grab them and put chains on them to load them into the wagons that take them to the ship."

"I don't blame them," said another. "People throw things at them and call them names as they are driven through town in those open wagons."

Elizabeth gathered the women around her and listened to their fears of the terrible journey and cruel treatment at the other end. Then she went to the Governor of the prison. She asked that the women be taken to the ship in closed carriages and without iron chains on their arms and legs.

"I want to go with them to the ship," she said. "If I am with them, they will go quietly." The Governor agreed and Elizabeth returned to the prisoners to tell them about her plans for their voyage. She spent the whole evening reading the Bible and praying with them.

The next morning, she was with them as they climbed calmly into the carriages. At the dock she went with them as they stepped quietly into the boats and were rowed to the dreaded ship. There Elizabeth had to persuade the captain that they would not try to jump overboard if they were allowed to stay on deck with her instead of being herded below and chained together in the dark hold.

Every day until the ship sailed, she went on board, reading and praying with them. She also organized them into groups with monitors of their choice to lead them. Each one was given a package containing such things as needles, colored threads, pins, thimble, scissors, comb, knife and fork, ball of string, apron, and a Bible. Especially important was a big bundle of material to make patchwork quilts. This would give them something to do as well as something they could sell wherever the ship stopped for fresh food and water. Since the quilts were something people wanted, the women would get a lot of money for them and would have money when they got to Australia. Also, being able to sew would help them get better jobs.

From that time on, no women prisoners left England without Elizabeth or another Friend going with them to the ship, giving them these supplies, and preparing them for the long voyage.

Many people admired and praised Elizabeth Fry. But there were also people who criticized her and made things hard for her. Some said that she neglected her own children and thought she shouldn't make the prisoners listen to Bible readings and prayers. But Elizabeth was sure in her heart that she was doing what God wanted her to do. She continued doing what she felt was right, always taking time to go to a person in trouble, counseling and praying with those who needed help and were seeking forgiveness. She was indeed "a light to the blind, speech to the dumb, and feet to the lame."

Sources for this story included Sara Corder's editing of Elizabeth Fry's *Journal* (Henry Longstreth, 1853); *A Faith to Live By* by Elfrida Vipont Foulds (Friends General Conference, 1963); *Builders of the Quaker Road* by Caroline Nicholson Jacobs (Regnery, 1953); *Elizabeth Fry* by Janet Whitney (Little Brown, 1936).

POPEYE, THE QUAKER MAN

By Carol Passmore

Setting: These events took place in 1990. They started when a girl in North Carolina didn't like something she saw on television.

Eowyn Evans punched the floor pillows once more, and then she was comfortable, ready to watch Saturday morning cartoons. She really enjoyed Saturdays, when her parents slept late and she got to watch some extra TV.

Suddenly, Eowyn sat up straight. Popeye, the Sailor Man, was eating Quaker oatmeal to get strong, and then he was punching out the aliens. He finished by singing his old song with new words, "I'm Popeye, the Quaker Man."

Eowyn scratched her head. She'd watched enough cartoons to know that Popeye always ate spinach, not oatmeal. Furthermore, although she had only been going to Quaker Meeting for three years, she had learned a lot about Quakers. She knew that Quakers believed in nonviolence. They didn't solve problems by punching the bad guy, whether he was an alien or the kid next door.

Eowyn, the Quaker girl, couldn't figure out what to do about Popeye, the Quaker man. She told her parents, who agreed that Popeye wasn't being very Quakerly, but they didn't seem interested in doing anything about it. She told her friends at school, but they didn't see what the problem was. Then she told her friends at First Day School at her Meeting. Some of them had seen the ads, and they agreed with Eowyn. They didn't like Popeye, the Quaker man. He wasn't only on TV, either. Some of the kids had found little comic books about Popeye in their cereal boxes, too.

"But what can we do about those ads?" asked Maggie. "We're just kids. Nobody listens to kids."

"Are we going to have Junior Meeting for Business next week?" Eowyn asked the First Day School teacher. "Because I'd like to write a letter to the Quaker Oats Company. Maybe all the kids can sign it."

"That's a good idea," said the teacher. "Maybe some kids will have ideas of other things to do too."

"OK," said Eowyn. "Everybody try to see the ads before then."

"Great," said Benjamin. "I'll tell my dad I have to watch TV."

When the children of Durham Monthly Meeting of Friends gathered on January 14, 1990, for Junior Meeting for Business, they had two items on the agenda. The first one was easy. They quickly decided to give the money they had earned, over $100, to the Heifer Project to buy animals to help poor families.

Then came the hard part, deciding what to do about Popeye. Eowyn read her letter, and then they discussed what to do. All the kids agreed that someone who was a Quaker, even Popeye, shouldn't solve problems by violence. But what could a few kids do?

"Maybe we should all stop eating Quaker oatmeal," said Flannery.

"That's called a boycott," said Nick, who was the oldest and was being Clerk of the Meeting for Business. "But that only works if lots of people do it. There are only 25 kids here."

"That's true," said Maggie. "Even if it's a boycott and a girlcott, there aren't enough of us."

"Maybe we could persuade a lot of other people to do it," suggested Hanna. "At least everybody in our schools."

"That wouldn't work at *my* school," Benjamin laughed. "Kids at my school like to punch a person out. Besides, they hate oatmeal."

"Does everyone agree that a boycott won't work?" asked Nick.

"Let's vote on it," said Pat.

"Quakers don't vote, either," said Nick. "They just try to find a solution everyone agrees with. I think we all agree a boycott won't work. So we need another idea."

"Maybe we should send a letter to the Quaker Oats Company," said Hanna, "but one that says more than Eowyn's letter says."

"Yes, one that uses all our ideas so it can be from the whole group," said Nick.

"They won't listen to a bunch of kids," warned Benjamin.

"Maybe we could tell them some ways to have Popeye act more like a Quaker," suggested David.

"And maybe they *will* listen to kids," said Eowyn.

All the children agreed to write a group letter telling how the entire group felt about the Popeye commercials. It wasn't easy writing a letter that said just what they wanted to say, but in two weeks they had a letter ready. This is what the letter said:

Dear Mr. Smithburg,

We are a group of children in Durham Friends Meeting. We have been greatly disturbed by your recent commercials showing Popeye describing himself as a Quaker or Quaker man and using violence against aliens, sharks, and Bluto. These actions are contrary to Quaker beliefs. Members of the Society of Friends believe violence should be avoided at all costs. We think that all living creatures have some of God in them. We are fearful of young impressionable viewers associating Quakerism with senseless violence. We feel that anyone calling him- or herself a Quaker should act like one and stick to Quaker philosophy. We suggest that Popeye display his strength in a more Quakerly manner, for example by rescuing children from a fire, supporting a breaking dam, or making friends with the aliens. Courage and strength can be shown in peaceful and helpful ways.

Sincerely,
The Children of
Durham Friends Meeting

All the children signed the letter, and they mailed copies of it to all the officers and members of the Board of the Quaker Oats Company. Eowyn's father had found a book with all the names in it. They also mailed a copy to the local newspaper.

On First Day two weeks later, the children found a letter waiting for them at the meetinghouse.

"Open it!" said Benjamin.

"I am," said Nick. "Don't be so impatient."

Nick opened the letter and read it out loud. It thanked the children for writing. Then it said, "We are sorry to learn that you were offended by the content of a recent advertisement for one of our products. Reactions and viewpoints of consumers are important to us. Please be assured that we will take your comments into consideration."

The kids were excited to have an answer to their letter. Some of them thought it meant the ads would stop playing on TV, but others pointed out that it didn't say so.

"I don't think they'll take the ads off," said Benjamin. "People don't listen to kids. We can't do anything to make a difference."

If that were the end of the story, Benjamin might have thought he was right, and kids can't make a difference. But a few other things happened because of the letter the children wrote.

First of all, Hanna's mother went to a committee meeting at the Friends General Conference office in Philadelphia. At the meeting there was a "show and tell" for grown-ups, and Hanna's mother shared the letter the children had written.

Second, a man named Russell Mitchell found a Popeye comic book in his cereal one morning. He wondered how Quakers felt about Popeye, the Quaker man. He wasn't a Quaker, but he knew about Quaker beliefs in nonviolence. So he called the Quaker office in Philadelphia to find out. He talked to Marty Walton, the General Secretary of Friends General Conference. She told him Quakers didn't like Popeye, the Quaker man at all. She also told him about the letter Hanna's

Written by the Willistown
M.M. First Day School
Drawn by Signe Wilkinson Landau

mother had shown her. So Russ Mitchell called the kids in Durham, too.

It was his job to wonder about things, because he was a reporter for *Business Week* magazine. He wrote an article that appeared in the magazine on March 12, 1990. In it he quoted the letter the children of Durham Friends Meeting had written. It was exciting to see an article in a national magazine about the kids in Durham Friends Meeting. The children began to wonder if perhaps they really were making a difference.

But that wasn't the end of Popeye. Lots of grown-up Quakers heard about the letter the kids had written, and wrote their own letters to the Quaker Oats Company. Some Quaker kids in Philadelphia liked the suggestion the Durham children had made in their letter for Popeye to use his strength in a helpful way. They drew cartoons of Popeye being helpful (see pages 130-131) and sent them to the Quaker Oats Company to be used to replace the comics in their cereal boxes.

Soon more and more people were complaining about Popeye. A Quaker woman in Philadelphia was on some radio talk shows. She told about the kids in Durham. She said not only was Popeye violent, but the ads were offensive to Quakers. "Would anyone advertise Popeye the Catholic man or Popeye the Jewish man?" she asked.

Then the Associated Press sent the story of the Durham kids' letter to newspapers all over the country. The children of Durham were excited to find themselves not only on the radio but in the newspapers as well.

Then a reporter from *The New York Times* called Durham. He arranged for some of the children to come to Hanna's house because she had a speaker phone. The kids all sat around the table and answered the reporter's questions. It was hard to remember to talk one at a time and say your name first when you spoke, but it was fun and challenging to tell the reporter about speaking out for something you believed.

As it turned out, *The New York Times* didn't print that story, because by that time the Quaker Oats Company had said they wouldn't run any more commercials where Popeye said he was a Quaker man. They said they wouldn't put any more of those comics in their cereal boxes either. But even without a story in *The New York Times*, the kids in Durham knew they had made a big difference.

STORIES OF THE UNDERGROUND RAILROAD

By Anna L. Curtis

Setting: In the years before slaves were freed in the United States, there were several escape routes for runaway slaves trying to get to Canada, where they would be safe. Families along the way would hide the runaways, feed them, and send them along to the next family in the chain. There was a law against helping slaves escape, and the families who helped them risked being jailed and made to pay a big fine if they were caught. Yet many families did help, and many thousands of people gained freedom this way. Here are two stories about the "Underground Railroad" on which they traveled.

Strawberries for Breakfast

One bright summer morning in southern Ohio, sunlight creeping across her face woke thirteen-year-old Lucinda Wilson at about five-thirty o'clock. She sat bolt upright, and then made a leap out of bed as she thought, "The strawberries on the hill must be ready to pick." Lucinda had been watching with eager eyes a hill overgrown with wild

---

Both "Strawberries for Breakfast" and "The Hearthstone" are from *Stories of the Underground Railroad*, compiled by Anna L. Curtis, New York: Island Press Cooperative, 1941. Adapted slightly and reprinted by permission of Fifteenth Street Monthly Meeting of the Religious Society of Friends.

strawberries. Now she joyously planned to surprise the family at breakfast with a basketful of the luscious, ripe berries.

She dressed rapidly but quietly so as not to disturb her sleeping sister. Lucinda had had the big bed to herself that night as her seventeen-year-old sister Mary was spending a few days with a friend on a nearby farm, and Ruth, the fifteen-year-old, slept on a narrow cot under the eaves at one end of the big upstairs room.

The Wilson house stood some distance back from the main road, with a long, straight drive from the gate to the front door. The drive seemed much too long, so Lucinda took a short-cut to the strawberry hill, which lay along the highway. It was a path leading out of the barnyard, almost invisible in the tangle of growth. Lucinda hurried along the path to the road, and started up the hill. There were the berries, just as red and delicious as she had hoped. She began to pick rapidly, but the bottom of her basket was not even covered when a voice called to her from the highway below.

Startled, she looked down and saw two men on horseback. They were strangers to her, and her first glance put her on guard, for her home was a station on the Underground Railroad. These men, she felt certain, were slave-catchers.

The next instant Lucinda knew she was right. The man who had called to her, dark and scowling, now spoke again, "Have you seen two black girls go past here?" he asked. "Two girls about seventeen or eighteen years old? They're only a few minutes ahead of us, we're sure."

Lucinda shook her head. She answered them honestly that she had just come to the spot, and had seen nobody but themselves.

The men touched their horses and moved on. But Lucinda had no more thought of berries. The two girls would come to her home, she was sure, and the men would catch them at the very door, unless they were warned. She looked cautiously after the riders, to make certain neither was glancing behind; then she darted across the road, and ran back along the path.

In a few moments, she was in the farmyard, and hurrying to the house. As she tore open the back door, she heard her mother's voice at the front. The girls had come, and the men would be there the next instant. Breathless, she burst upon them. The door was still open, the girls and her mother standing in the hall.

"Shut the door! Shut the door quick!" she gasped. "They're coming!"

Even as she spoke, she saw a horse turn into the driveway. Her mother slammed the door, locked it, and looked wildly around for a hiding-place for the two trembling girls, who were starting to wail that they would be dragged back again, sure, and would never be free.

"Hush!" said Emily Wilson. "Go upstairs. Quick!"

They rushed up the stairs, and into the room where Ruth was now up and half-dressed. She looked up, startled, as the four burst in.

"Lucinda," her mother directed, "put on thy night-cap and night-gown again, and get into bed."

She seized Mary's night-clothes from under the pillow, and thrust them upon one of the runaways.

"Put these on, and get into bed with my daughter. Lie next the wall, and turn thy head away from the door. Pull the cap well down over thy face."

As the girls hastened to obey, Emily Wilson lifted the top of a large square wicker clothes-hamper which stood at the side of the room. Fortunately, it was nearly empty.

"Get in there," she said to the other girl, who stepped in and crouched down for the lid to be replaced.

A loud knock sounded at the front door. "Sit on the basket, Ruth, and catch thy dressing-gown around thee. The slave-catchers will be up here in a moment."

Emily Wilson glanced around the room. There was nothing in sight to show that the runaways had been there, and she hastened down the stairs to open the door.

"Good morning, ma'am," said one of the men. "We're after those two slave girls that you have here."

"Indeed," she answered, "and how does thee know that we have two slave girls here?"

"Because we were right on their heels, and we know they wouldn't have gone past here. So you'll have to let us search the house."

"You are welcome to do so, if you wish. But I can assure you that it will be wasted labor."

"We'll see about that," answered the man, as the two began a thorough search of each room in the house. Emily Wilson let them open the doors, and look as they would, until they came to the girls' room. Then she stepped forward.

"My three daughters sleep there," she said, "and it is yet early morning. Gentlemen, I beg you not to enter their room."

"Just as likely to be here as anywhere," said one of the men, and he opened the door and went in.

There were the three girls, two in bed, with the bed-clothes pulled up to their ears; the other sitting upon the wicker hamper, holding her wrapper about her, as though taken by surprise. In the hamper under her, however, the terrified runaway was trembling so that it seemed to Ruth the men must see the hamper shaking. She sat as heavily as she could, and covered the hamper with her wrapper as far as possible.

Somewhat embarrassed, the men looked hastily about the room, opened the closet-door, and finding nothing, went out again, with a half-hearted apology.

"Well," said one of them, as they came from the last room, "it begins to look as though those girls went past here, after all. We'd better put on speed, and perhaps we can overtake them yet."

"I told you it would be wasted labor," said Emily Wilson, quietly. She then hospitably offered them breakfast, but they refused in their haste. They galloped off and the girls were free to come from their hiding-places. . . .

"I'm glad I decided to pick strawberries for breakfast," said Lucinda. "And it's still early enough for me to go back and fill my basket. We'll have some for breakfast, after all."

The two girls stayed quietly in the house all day. Late that night a covered wagon took them to another Quaker home on another road. From there they were sent on the next day with little danger, for word had come back that the two slave-catchers had lost all trace of them and declared that they had burrowed underground.

The Hearthstone

The three Murrays sat around their pleasant fire, each busily occupied. Hannah Murray, by the light of a candle, turned the heel of the woolen yarn stocking she was knitting. Her husband John, with another candle on the little stand beside him, read aloud from *The Anti-Slavery Standard*. Eleven-year-old Richard shook a long-handled skillet full of popcorn which he held over the coals, and listened happily to the sound of its popping.

"Here is the account of a slave-sale in Charleston," said Richard's father. "Mothers separated from their children, husbands from their wives. It is terrible work," he sighed, "but it cannot last. . . ."

As he spoke, there was the sound of feet on the porch, and a knock at the door. John Murray laid down his paper, went to the door, and opened it.

"So you are home, are you?" was the officious greeting which came from outside.

"Yes," answered John Murray, gravely. "I am at home. Is there anything else that thee would like to know?"

"Not just now," was the visitor's reply. As he spoke, he brushed past John Murray, and glanced into the living-room. Richard and his mother looked up in surprise, and the man stepped back to the door.

"Everybody is at home here," he said to his companions outside, and the party left the porch, with a word of thanks to John Murray who in deep thought closed the door, dropped a heavy bar across it, and came back to his seat.

This happened in Ohio, about the year 1856. The Murrays and practically all their neighbors were strongly opposed to slavery. Whenever the marshals were on the track of an escaped slave, there were half a dozen Quaker homes here which were sure to be searched, and first of all the home of John and Hannah Murray.

John looked thoughtful as he resumed his reading. After a few moments a second knock, much louder, sounded on the door. He sprang to his feet and looked at his wife.

"They have been to the stable and found the horses gone. Now they are sure there are slaves in the settlement, and they will search the house." He turned to the windows, and pulled down the shades, while Hannah Murray dropped a cone-shaped tin extinguisher over the flame of each of the candles.

"We are caught," said John Murray. "There is only one thing to do."

His wife darted from the room, while he spoke to the boy, who was excitedly watching the door.

"Richard, go upstairs, and wait until I call thee down. Then come quickly, and pop corn again, as though nothing had happened. Keep on popping, even though we do have visitors."

Richard hurried up the stairs. As he reached the top, he stopped in amazement, as he caught a glimpse of his mother coming quickly back to the living-room, leading a Negro by the hand.

"What is wanted?" Richard's father was calling to the men outside.

"You know very well what is wanted," came the reply. "We are after a fugitive slave. Open the door, or we shall break it in!"

"If you are peaceable, I will gladly let you in," answered John Murray, and he and his wife hurried the Negro into the room where they had just been sitting.

Richard stared in surprise from the top of the stairs. He knew that his father had not intended that he should see this, but he could not turn his eyes away, though he determined to let no word escape him to show where the fugitive might be. Where could they hide him in the room anyway? There were no closets, nor large pieces of furniture which might conceal him.

As the boy stood puzzling, his father softly called him, and he hastened down the stairs, hearing all the while a rain of blows on the stout house-door. He hurried into the room, and glanced about. There was no sign of the Negro. His mother was lighting the candles again with a "spill," or lighter, from the vase of tapers on the mantel. The cat, which had been sleeping in a chair, was now curled up on the hearthstone close to where Richard himself had been standing. Where was the slave? But even as he wondered, he took up his skillet of popcorn and held it over the fire.

Outside, there was a shout, "Now, boys, all together!" There was a rush, and John Murray threw open the door, just as three men plunged against it and fell headlong into the room, one of them breaking a chair as he fell.

The three rose quickly in much ill-temper. "We want that slave, Mr. Murray, and we mean to have him," said the leader. "Here's a warrant for his arrest."

"We have no slaves here, my friend; none but free people—as free as thee, and with much better manners. And as for thy warrant—where is thy warrant for breaking my furniture?"

"Search the house, boys," said the leader. "Don't pay any attention to him."

"Give them a light, Hannah. Let them look; let them search thoroughly." This was spoken with a calm smile.

Hannah Murray handed a lighted candle to the men. "You should be proud of your business," she said. "You should be proud of chasing poor black people over the country, to carry them back to slavery."

The men hurried about their search, and the tramp of their feet sounded along the halls, and from room to room over the house. John and Hannah Murray took their seats again, and looked soberly into the fire, while Richard, upon the hearthstone, popped his corn carefully, although it was all he could do to keep from shouting with excitement.

Through the bedrooms, the kitchen, and the cellar the searchers went, but found no sign of the runaway; they muttered a few words of apology and left the house again. Hannah Murray took the candle from them saying gently, as she closed the door:

"What would your mothers think if they knew you had descended to such work as this?"

The clatter of horses' hoofs sounded on the road. The men were gone. Richard could no longer contain himself.

"What did thee do with him, Father?" he cried. "Where did thee hide him?"

"So thee watched?" asked his father.

"I didn't mean to; but Mother came in with him before I was upstairs."

"Perhaps thee should know, now; but first let me see if any of our visitors remain on the porch or nearby." John Murray stepped out, and looked carefully around. Finding nobody, he returned to the room.

"Now, Richard," he said with a smile. "I think thee has popped corn enough. Step off the hearthstone, and lift old

Tabby back to her chair. Did thee wonder how she came to get down on the hearthstone?"

"A little, but I was thinking more about the man."

"I lifted her down myself," said his father, turning back the rag carpet from the half of the hearthstone which it covered. "Now help me move the stone."

Together they turned the stone back. Here was exposed the entrance to a dark but roomy home beneath the floor of the house. A small ladder was provided for descending. Several people might be comfortably hidden in the recess while search went on over their heads.

Richard peered in eagerly, while his father called: "Samuel."

"Can I come up now?" came a voice from the darkness below.

John Murray held a candle over the hole. Richard was amazed that here in his own house was such a hideaway that his own exploring curiosity had not led him to discover before. How could it have been made without his knowledge? Perhaps at night while he was asleep. He looked at his father with beaming admiration.

Now he was big enough to be a part of the Railroad!

Samuel came quickly to the surface, and the hearthstone and carpet were replaced. Then John Murray said:

"Samuel, thee should know my boy Richard, who stood on the hearthstone above thee, with this cat sleeping beside him, and so turned the search away from this room."

The fugitive turned toward the boy, but Richard spoke quickly to stop the thanks which were coming. "I didn't know that I was doing it, but I'm glad if I did help."

A BOLD NEW PLAN

By Mary Esther McWhirter and Janet Sabina

Setting: Only thirty years after the American Revolution, the United States fought England and Canada again. When the war was finally over, there was a lot of mistrust and fear on both sides of the border.

Richard Rush sat in his office in the U.S. State Department in Washington, reading a letter. He frowned. He shook his head. He laid the letter on his desk and looked out his office window. The great dome of the new capitol building shone in the afternoon sunlight. The United States of America was less than forty years old. As countries go, it was very, very young. Its dreams of freedom and opportunity for all were still very new.

"At last we have peace!" he sighed. "I pray we never fight England and our Canadian neighbors again."

Richard Rush picked up the letter and read it a second time. It was from an army officer on duty along the Canadian border. It said, "The United States government must send soldiers to take the place of those recently withdrawn from the Canadian border."

Based on material from *Peace Crusaders*, compiled by Anna Bassett Griscom for American Friends Service Committee, J.B. Lippincott Co., 1928.

"No!" thought Richard Rush. "Armies stationed along a border bring war, not peace."

The letter went on, "Of course we will need American battleships to guard the Great Lakes."

"No!" thought Richard Rush. "Ships bristling with guns create fear between countries. What we need is trust."

The letter said, "Larger forts with thicker walls are needed if our beloved United States is to be safe."

"I love my country as much as the army officer who wrote this letter," thought Richard Rush. "I know most countries think soldiers and battleships and forts are needed to keep their borders safe. But we need a better way. I have another plan. It just may work. At least, it's worth trying."

He pushed his chair back from his desk and left his office. He walked quickly to the office of the British Ambassador, Sir Charles Bagot. Sir Charles was in charge of Canadian affairs in the United States since Canada was still an English colony.

"Sir Charles," said Richard Rush, "I have received a letter from one of our officers on duty on our border with Canada. He calls for larger forts, more battleships, more soldiers. It seems to me that that will just cause more trouble and mistrust on both sides."

"That is just exactly what I've been thinking," responded Sir Charles. "The two peoples should be friends, not enemies."

We do not know all that was said that afternoon. But we do know that Richard Rush and Sir Charles Bagot outlined a bold new plan, the likes of which had never been seen before. They made three proposals: bring home the soldiers, withdraw the battleships, destroy the forts. That would mean leaving the whole boundary unarmed and undefended.

Of course, there were violent objections on both sides of the border. This sort of thing had never been done before. Everyone had always assumed that borders needed to be defended, especially when there had been fights in the past and the people didn't trust each other. Now, on both sides of the Canadian border, people inquired anxiously, "How do we know they won't attack us if we give up our defenses?"

It took a lot of patience and six whole years to work it out. Leaders met again and again asking questions and listening to answers. They discussed the plan and revised it, and then revised it again. At last, in 1818, a treaty was signed. It still said *no* soldiers, *no* battleships, *no* forts along the border. It was called the Rush-Bagot Agreement for the two people who had first had the imagination and courage to suggest it.

A hundred years went by. From time to time, disagreements between the two countries came up. There were even quarrels, when people got pretty excited and called each other names. Some of the arguments were about where the boundary should be. The parts above Maine and the western part of the United States hadn't been decided yet when the treaty was signed.

But each time the dispute was settled around a conference table with words instead of on a battlefield with swords or guns. Today, the boundary stretches all the way across the continent—three thousand miles—without a single fort or soldier or battleship to guard it.

In 1918, Canadians and Americans celebrated the first one hundred years of peace between them. At Blaine, Washington, near the western end of the border, they built a gate. Half of the gate was in the United States; half of it was in Canada. At the top, in the middle, they put two flagpoles, one for each country's flag. Inside the arch of the gate, they carved these words:

Open for One Hundred Years.
May These Borders Never Be Closed.

Most people today have never even heard of the Rush-Bagot Agreement, but their bold new plan worked, and that's the important thing. Most people don't even know that Canadians and the citizens of the United States were once enemies. Maybe that's just as well.

CHRIST OF THE ANDES

By Mary Esther McWhirter

I t was the week before Easter, 1900. In Argentina great throngs of people went to church every day. With words and songs they honored Jesus, the Prince of Peace.

Across the Andes mountains, in Chile, great throngs of people also went to church every day. With words and songs, they too honored Jesus, the Prince of Peace.

But when they were not in church, men and women in both Argentina and Chile were busily preparing for war. Gunboats were built and forts constructed. Fathers and older brothers were called away from their work on the farms and in the factories. Day by day they marched and drilled, learning how to be soldiers. Children had less food than usual. When their shoes wore out, they had to go barefoot. Even after their clothes became ragged, they went right on wearing them. And all because the money usually spent for food, shoes, and clothes was being spent for guns, cannon, and warships.

On both sides of the Andes mountains there were angry words and threats as hatred mounted. The reason for the quarreling between the two countries was disagreement about

Based on "Christ of the Andes" by Anna D. White, *Peace Crusaders*, compiled by Anna Bassett Griscom for American Friends Service Committee, J. B. Lippincott Company, 1928. *Books of Goodwill*, Vol 1, National Council for the Prevention of War. Used by permission of the author, Mary Esther McWhirter.

the location of the boundary line separating them. When the leaders from Argentina and Chile met to talk things over, they fell into angry disputes. Chile probably said something like this: "Argentina, you do not own all that river. Just remember that it rises here in Chile. So we have a perfect right to use it to turn the wheels of our mills."

The representative from Argentina may have retorted, "And you tell your miners to stay away from our part of the mountains!"

"Your part of the mountains! We'll have you know that those peaks belong to Chile."

"They do not. Our big guns will teach your miners to stay on their own side of the line."

No doubt, this warning from Argentina called forth a heated reply from Chile: "We, too, have guns and we'll use them to prove just exactly where that line really is!"

Such talk by their leaders brought great sadness to many of the citizens of both countries, among them Bishop Benavente of Buenos Aires. All during the week before Easter he listened gravely, his heart deeply troubled by the probability of war. Then, when Easter Sunday came and the great cathedral was filled with worshipers, he preached a sermon that his people never forgot.

"Oh, my people, I beg of you—stop building warships and drilling armies. That is not the way to peace. Suppose Argentina and Chile do go to war. Killing the fathers and older brothers in the two countries will not decide where the boundary line is. Fighting will not tell us which country is right. It will only tell us which has the bigger army and the more powerful guns. Let us ask the King of England to hear both sides and tell us what to do. Let us be friends with our neighbors the Chileans. Let us remember the teachings of Jesus, the Prince of Peace, whom we honor on this Easter Day."

When the news of this Easter sermon reached Bishop Java of Chile, he proclaimed the same message to his people. "We call ourselves followers of the Prince of Peace," he said. "Let us then work not for war, but for peace."

In the weeks that followed, Bishop Benavente traveled about on foot, from city to city in Argentina, preaching good will and Christian love for all people. On the other side of the Andes mountains, in Chile, Bishop Java traveled about on foot, from city to city, preaching good will and Christian love for people everywhere. In both countries people gathered to listen. They went away to work and pray for peace. They made their wishes clear to their rulers.

Once again the rulers met. This time they sent a message to the King of England saying, "Your Majesty, we implore you to help us settle our disagreement without going to war."

After sending surveyors to the Andes mountains to get all the facts, the King divided the land that had caused the threat of war. In both countries there was great rejoicing. "Now we can go home to our farms and factories!" exclaimed the soldiers of Argentina.

"Now we can use the money that might have been spent for guns and cannon and warships to buy food and shoes and clothes for our children!" cried the fathers of Chile.

People started saying, "Now there is money to build a railroad between the capital city of Chile, Santiago, and the capital of Argentina, Buenos Aires." Then the engineers made plans that would make it possible for the people of the two cities to travel back and forth across the Andes mountains.

As Bishop Benavente saw the good things that were happening, he was deeply thankful that the people of both lands had chosen the way of peace rather than the way of war. It was a choice that he wanted them to remember always. So he wrote a letter that was published far and wide. In the letter he said: "Let us hire the young sculptor, Senor Alonso, to make a statue of Christ. We can make the statue out of the bronze cannons that we were going to use for war."

The bishop's idea spread like wildfire. Money poured in, given gladly by the people of both lands. After the great statue was finished, it was carried to a point near the Upsallata Pass, nearly 13,000 feet above sea level. The first part of the journey was by train, the next part by mule. Soldiers and sailors dragged the heavy statue the last bit of the way where no railroad car or mule could travel.

Then came the day for raising the statue—March 13, 1904. Over 3,000 people made the long, slow climb to the top of the mountain. That night the ones from Argentina camped on the Chilean side, while the ones from Chile camped on the Argentinian side. This was to show that they were friends and trusted each other.

Next day, when the statue of Christ was unveiled, bands played the national anthems of the two countries. Shouts and cheers for the two presidents echoed and re-echoed from mountain peak to mountain peak. Worship, led by churchmen from the two countries, was followed by speeches made by statesmen. No one who was there could ever forget the moment when, at sunset time, men, women, and children knelt down to pray for a world at peace. As the last rays of the sun shone against the snowy peaks, Bishop Carlos of Chile spoke the final words of dedication:

Sooner shall these mountains crumble into dust than Argentines and Chileans break the peace sworn at the feet of Christ the Redeemer.

In 1937 a bronze tablet, inscribed with these words, was placed on the monument. Today, many years later, the statue is still there, and the people of Argentina and Chile are still at peace.

EXPERIMENT IN FAIRNESS

By Bayard Rustin

Setting: Bayard Rustin was an African American leader who worked for the
Fellowship of Reconciliation (FOR) for equal rights for all Americans during
the civil rights efforts of the 1960s. When he wrote this story, the terms
colored and *Negro* were in common use.

Between speaking engagements in a Midwestern college
town I went into a small restaurant to buy a hamburger
and a glass of milk. I had not been sitting in the
restaurant long before I noticed that I was being ignored. After
waiting about ten minutes I decided that the conflict had to be
faced. I moved to one corner, stood directly before a waitress so
that she could not overlook me, and said, "I would like to have
a hamburger."

"I'm sorry," she replied, "but we can't serve . . . er, er . . .
you, er . . . colored people here."

"Who's responsible for this?" I asked.

She made her reply in two gestures—the first indicating a
woman standing in the rear; and the second, a finger to the lip,
an obvious appeal for me not to involve her in any way.

Reprinted by permission of The Fellowship of Reconciliation, Box 271, Nyack, NY
10960.

I walked directly to the woman standing near the coffee urn in the rear of the restaurant. "I would like to know why it is impossible for me to be served here?" I asked.

"Well . . . well, er . . ." she stuttered, "it's . . . er . . . it's because we don't do that in this town. They don't serve colored people in any of the restaurants."

"Why?" I asked.

"It's because they're dirty," she said, "and they won't work, and because if I served them everybody would walk out, and then what would happen to my business?"

I took from my pocket a report by the local FOR. It explained many actual facts about juvenile delinquency, unemployment, boisterousness, and other conditions and qualities that many people thought were especially typical of Negroes. Together, we went through those facts. One by one, we eliminated all the problems that would interfere with my being served, except the economic one.

"Have you ever served Negroes?" I asked.

"No," she replied warily.

"Then why do you believe that doing so would upset your customers?" I then appealed to her to make an experiment in the extension of democracy. After some hesitation she agreed to the following terms: that I would sit in the front of the restaurant for ten minutes, during which time I would not eat my hamburger. We would count the number of people who left or did not come in because of me. If we saw one such person I would leave myself. If we did not, I could eat my hamburger.

I waited fifteen minutes. Then she approached me, picked up the cold hamburger, placed a hot one before me, and said simply, "What will you have to drink with it?"

I have been given to understand by Negroes and whites who live in that town that Mrs. Duffy continues to serve Negroes without embarrassment or conflict, which is indeed a courageous thing in the circumstances.

NEW GIRL IN SCHOOL

By Carol Passmore

W hat can I tell you except that I was pretty excited about the first day of school. I'd been the new kid the year before and had worked really hard at being popular. I don't mean to brag, but I had been fairly successful.

I picked my clothes days ahead and changed my mind four times that morning. Finally, I was standing with my friends in front of High Point Central High on a beautiful sunny morning in September, 1959, eager to begin my junior year.

"So," said Annette, "we decided we'll be nice to her."

"Who?" I asked, realizing that I had been daydreaming.

"To the nigger who's coming to school," said Annette. "The principal says we aren't going to have any trouble like they did in Little Rock."

Lib giggled."Then you had better not call her a nigger."

"Sure," I said. "I think we should be nice to her." I hadn't really thought about our school being desegregated. Besides, High Point Central High was a big school. I'd probably never see her anyway.

I was wrong about that. Her name was Lynn and she was in my first period algebra class, sitting quietly in the back of the room, and in my second period English class, sitting quietly in the front. I didn't know where she went third period, but in fourth period history, she was sitting right beside me.

I didn't hear too much the teacher said, because somehow I got the idea that I would show her where the cafeteria was. I wondered if that would be considered being "too nice," but I also remembered my first lunch alone the year before. So when the bell rang, I politely offered Lynn a guided tour to the lunchroom.

By the time we went to our lockers—hers was near mine—and then to the cafeteria, there was a long line. Everyone got quiet when we joined it. After we got our meatloaf and lumpy mashed potatoes, I could see that the tables were getting full and I didn't see any space with Lib and the others. I spotted a half-empty table with some kids I didn't know and we sat there.

Instantly, those kids all got up and left, so Lynn and I had eight extra chairs in that jammed cafeteria. But it was obvious that no one was going to join us.

There we sat, like two kids on a deserted island, in the middle of that crowded cafeteria. I stared at Lynn and she stared at me. Her short black hair was wavy and her skin was a rich coppery brown. My brown hair was short and wavy and my skin, with its summer tan, was almost as brown as hers. I figured we could pass as sisters.

Lynn poked at the disgusting-looking meat loaf. "You don't have to eat with me," she said. "You can go and eat with your friends."

I stirred my peas into my potatoes while I thought about that. "If they don't want to come and eat with us," I muttered, "I'm not sure they're my friends."

So I stayed, and for all of our junior and senior years, Lynn and I ate lunch together. There was lots of good in those years, and plenty that wasn't so good.

Lynn and I never had to hunt for a table in the cafeteria. We had our own private table right in the middle. The bad part was no one else ever worked up the courage to join us.

Another good thing was that my friends and a lot of other kids were polite to Lynn. The bad part was that they were polite to me also. When I bumped into Lib in the bathroom one day, she explained. "When we said 'friendly,' we didn't mean that friendly."

Some kids called us names and occasionally threw things at us, but nothing serious. To look on the bright side, there wasn't anyone in the school who didn't know who we were.

Another good thing was that after a few weeks of talking about what had happened in our classes that day, Lynn and I discovered that we had lots in common. Besides having almost all the same classes, we also had the same interests. If fate hadn't thrown us together, we'd probably have met and become good friends anyway.

Probably the best thing about those two years was that I met some people who worked for the American Friends Service Committee. They taught Lynn and me about nonviolence and helped us be nice to the people who called us names. They also introduced us to some other people in North Carolina who didn't think that the color of your skin should determine where you went to school or what job you could have. We had lots of fun with these people, too, which made up for the fact that we weren't involved in many of the high school social activities.

Sometimes now I think about these years and get out my old high school year books. In my sophomore year book, when I was working at being popular, lots of kids signed my book, saying how nice I was. In my junior year, only a few kids signed my book, and all they wrote was how they enjoyed being in my English class or algebra class, but nothing about me.

My senior year, they wrote different things. All those popular kids I had wanted for my friends wanted to sign my year book. They wrote how much they admired someone who would stand up for what she believed was right. They didn't say they had changed their minds about race relations, and I'm not sure being admired made up for being lonely and left out, but I was glad they were willing to sign.

But the best one was from Lynn, who wrote a whole page. She wrote how scared she had been on that first day and how glad she had been when I spoke to her. I was surprised, because she hadn't looked scared at all, but then, you don't know everything about your best friend.

MADAME MARIE

By Odette Meyers

Setting: In World War II, all Jews in countries controlled by the Nazis had to wear a yellow "Star of David" so everyone would know they were Jews. Thousands of Jews were rounded up and taken away to their death. People who were caught helping them were killed too. But some people cared enough to protect Jews from capture. This is a woman's own story of how she was saved when she was seven years old.

On July 16, the Nazis struck, and 13 thousand stateless Jews in Paris were rounded up by the French police. . . . Among the 13 thousand . . . there were 4,051 children. If it had not been for the woman who saved me, I would have been number 4,052.

The concièrge[1] was a woman named Marie Chotel, whom everyone in the neighborhood loved and affectionately called "Madame Marie." She lived downstairs from us. There was a kind of corridor between her apartment and the front door. One day, at about five o'clock in the morning, she ran up, yanked us out of bed and said, "They are coming for you!" She threw us quickly into her apartment and put us, my mother and me, into a broom closet and closed the door. When we had gotten out of bed, we had grabbed clothing that had the yellow star on

---

[1] *The concièrge is the manager of the apartment house.*

From *The Courage to Care* by Carol Ritter and Sondra Myers (Eds.), New York: New York University Press, 1986. Reprinted by permission.

it. So while we were in the closet standing up, my mother, for some reason, was trying to unstitch the star.

The search team came in, and Madame Marie immediately, with all her peasant shrewdness, put on a terrific act of being . . . the local gossip. . . . When she was greeted by the search team she said, "How wonderful that you are clearing France of all Jews. I'm so honored that you have come here. Please have a glass of wine."

They kept asking for us, and she exclaimed, "Oh, those Jews. You know how they are. They live in poor places like this, but they all have money. They have gone off to their country home. I can't afford it. But they certainly can." She carried on and on that way, and they believed her. She kept pouring them more wine. . . .

Madame Marie's husband, who was called "Monsieur Henri" by everyone, was a member of the underground. [After the search team left] he was fetched from his job and he came immediately. Monsieu Henri was a big man. I was quite small, only seven. We walked outside. There were German soldiers everywhere. I remember that. He held my hand. I was trembling. My hand was shaking. I remember that there were trucks full of Jews being rounded up, and he told me, "Remember, look at your feet and keep on walking." It was like the refrain to children from the whole occupied Paris. "If anyone calls you don't answer. Don't look up. Don't answer." So we walked like that. Nobody called. And I looked at my feet as we walked. We reached the subway entrance, and I remember a wonderful sense of safety as I went down into the subway. I was saved, and hidden by Catholics because this man took me to safety.

The subway station was almost deserted, and we had to wait for a metro, a subway train, to take us to the railway station. There we met with other children and a gentile woman who was to accompany us to our hiding place in the country. It was prearranged by the Resistance. . . . I ended up in a Catholic village for the duration of the occupation. . . .

Madame Marie had a very simple philosophy. We were Jewish and she did not want to impose her religion on us, but she told me a story. "The heart is like an apartment," she said, "and if it's messy and there is nothing to offer, no food or drink to offer guests, nobody will want to come. But is it's clean and dusted every day, and if it's pretty and there are flowers and food and drink for guests, people will want to come and they will want to stay for dinner. And if it's super nice, God himself will want to come." That was it.

Whenever I would do something wrong, she would put me on a high stool facing the wall, and she would say to me, "I think you have some housework to do." It was my business to figure out how I had messed up my heart in some way. I had to get a broom and dust pan and get to work. That was her philosophy and what she taught me. It has been important all through my life.

In every single situation, each time, she did what she had told me to do: to do a dusting and a cleaning of my heart every day, to see to it that everything was all right. She saved not only my life—my physical life— but my spirit also.

There is a Jewish proverb that I love. It says, "If you are in a place where there is no human being, *be* a human being." I think the business of being a full human being takes a lot of energy and a lot of strong thinking, and that you must think things through by yourself, based on your own experience. That's what I learned from Madame Marie.

SANCTUARY MEANS LOVE

Setting: This story is by a member of one Friends Meeting which, like many other faith communities in the 1980s, gave protection and support through the Sanctuary Movement to refugees fleeing the violence in Central America. The names and locations have been changed because when this story was written the Meeting was still giving Sanctuary to the same refugees.

The call came late one night, from a Friend on the west coast. "Would your Friends Meeting be able to give sanctuary to a family of six?" he asked.

"That's a lot of people!" I exclaimed. "And we're a small meeting."

"I know, but two young couples and their month-old babies, fleeing from violence in Guatemala, need your support and protection. You must decide quickly!" He continued, "They need help fast. One of the babies is stranded with her parents on the Mexican side of the border. We're worried that the child isn't getting enough to eat and may be starving to death. We need to know if someone from your Meeting could travel to the border to help these refugees cross," he went on, "and if you think all six refugees can come and live in sanctuary with your Meeting."

As I put down the phone, I thought about how our Meeting had decided to become a Sanctuary. For several years, members had been concerned about the terrible violence in Central America. We heard daily reports of hundreds and thousands of people fleeing from the fighting around them and from arrest and torture by their governments. Where could these men, women, and children go?

We Quakers went to sleep safely in warm, comfortable beds each night and woke up safely each morning. We began to think about sharing this security with at least one or two refugees by doing something that meetings, churches, and synagogues in other parts of the United States and Canada were doing—giving sanctuary to Central American refugees. Yet we knew that giving sanctuary involved risk and hard work. We would be breaking a national law, and it would take lots of help from lots of people.

Our Meeting held a special Meeting for Worship to consider becoming a Sanctuary. Friends spoke out of the silence. "We might be breaking our government's law, but we would be following God's law to help people in trouble," one Friend said. "There aren't many of us and we aren't rich, but isn't God calling on us to share what we have?" asked another. Using an old Quaker phrase, one older woman reasoned, "If God means us to accept this challenge, *way will open.* I think we should go ahead."

So when the call came that night, our Meeting had already decided to become a Sanctuary for Central American refugees. "But are we really ready and able to provide care and support for six people," I wondered. "And who would be able to go to the border to help the baby and her parents get across safely?" Now that six real human beings needed our help, would the way really open? My husband John and I talked long into the night.

In the morning, we called together the Meeting Sanctuary Committee and shared our news. The Committee decided that one member should be supported to go to the border to help with the crossing. We would discuss next steps later. Right now, we would meet this most urgent need. John, who speaks fluent Spanish and had worked with refugees, was asked to go.

John flew west, thousands of miles to the border. I waited at home for the call that all were safe. The danger for a United States citizen helping someone cross the border illegally was arrest, trial, and possible fine and imprisonment. John went knowing that if this happened to him, his family and the Meeting would be there to help.

We all knew that the danger for the refugees was far greater. If they were caught entering the country, they could be put in prison and sent back to Guatemala. At the time, we didn't know why Carlos, the young father, had left Guatemala. Later, he told us he had been arrested four times during high school for speaking against his government. The last time, he narrowly escaped being killed. If he was sent back to Guatemala, Carlos would almost certainly be imprisoned and might be killed. Where would that leave his young wife Maria and baby Anna? The border crossing had to be very secret and very careful.

John finally called, his voice full of joy and excitement. All were safely across. An all-night celebration was in progress. The two baby cousins, a boy and a girl, were being happily passed back and forth. "I'll tell you more when I get home," he concluded.

It was quite a story. Carlos and Maria had tried to cross the border once before Anna was born but had almost been caught. Life on the Mexican side of the border was very difficult and dangerous for refugees. Carlos could not even look for work. Finally they found shelter with Mexicans who were part of the Sanctuary Movement. There Anna was born, but mother and child were too weak to travel at first. Food was very scarce, and without enough food, Maria didn't have enough breast milk for her baby. They had to travel away from the border, where they found temporary food and shelter. Finally, they were strong enough to try to cross the border again.

When John arrived, he rented a jeep and drove through winding roads to the lonely border meeting place. He waited tensely on his side of the fence for hours, aware with each passing minute that the drive back to town would be more dangerous the darker it became. But the family's trip to the meeting place on their side of the border was long and hard. They had to walk several miles to get there, and it was already dark by the time they arrived.

First to be passed over the fence was the baby, Anna. She began to scream, grabbed John's beard, and pulled hard. John had all he could do to keep from screaming himself. Maria crossed next. Carlos came in at a different place and was met by someone else, as that was the safest way.

John bundled the tired mother and child into the jeep and began to drive cautiously back to town. He was all too aware that in the dark he could see only the lights of other cars. The border police could be in those cars, and he wouldn't know it until they pulled him over. Then what would he say?

Though frightened himself, John tried to speak to Maria during the trip. She remained silent, huddled in the corner with her sleeping baby in her arms. Imagine how frightened she must have been, driving through the dark in a new country, with a man she did not know, a bearded Quaker! But the trip went without incident, and Maria and Anna were delivered safely into Carlos' arms. Only then did Maria relax and give John a shy smile.

By the time John returned home, way had opened for all six refugees to come into our Sanctuary. Some Friends worked several Saturdays to prepare space in the home of one member of the Meeting. Others began the difficult job of planning round-the-clock helpers to stay with the families when they first arrived. We planned how to get food and clothing for them, and we all practiced our Spanish.

In the meantime, the two families rested and enjoyed some time together after their long separation. Then they began the long trip across the United States, driving many miles each night and staying with different Sanctuary familes along the way.

The way it worked was that each family they stayed with would call ahead to the next place and say, "The lone ranger is here." Then those people would gather clothes and food, get their cars fueled up, and be ready to drive the refugees to the next place. Thus they came on a modern "undergound railroad" not very different from the one used by escaping slaves over a hundred years before.

John and I borrowed a van to bring them the last part of the journey. We woke at 5 AM to set out over the mountains. It was a fine April morning. We arrived at the Sanctuary safe-house just as everyone was having breakfast. We all sat on the back porch, drank coffee, and passed around those beautiful babies.

As I write this, Anna is four years old. She has a beautiful baby brother named David. Her family has brought so much to our Meeting! They have cared for our children, taught us how to cook Guatemalan food, and shared their music and poetry at many celebrations. We have worked together to plan vigils, prayer services, and other events to help others in our community and state to understand the situation in Central America. There have been times of fear and difficulty, misunderstanding, and hurt feelings. But over and over again, we work and listen and struggle with each other, and finally, way opens and we can take a next step in our experiment of caring for each other in Sanctuary.

(The United States Congress finally passed a law that was supposed to keep refugees from being sent back, but it didn't always work. Also, it only protected them for two years, and it didn't include Guatemalans. So in the eary 1990s most refugees were still in danger, and so were the people who tried to help them. Some Quakers and people of other faiths had been arrested for their work in the Sanctuary Movement. But Friends and others continued to work for the right of all people to enter this country with full rights as human beings.)

WHO SAID IT CAN'T HAPPEN HERE?

By Elinor Briggs

Setting: When the United States and Japan were at war in the 1940s, many Americans were afraid that the Japanese Americans in California might help the Japanese invade our country. So hundreds of Americans of Japanese ancestry were taken from their homes and put in camps until the war was over. Many years later, the United States government said this had been unfair, and money was given to families who had been put in the camps.

Seji looked across the field of cantaloupe. It was a beautiful sight: a dark green field, full of ripening melons, nearly ready for harvest. Last year had been a good year, and this crop promised to be even better, perhaps even good enough to pay off the last bit of money his family still owed for this piece of land.

Seeing the soft breeze stir the leaves of the vines, Seji remembered how little he was when his father had taken him to see the land before he tried to buy it. The land had been for sale for many years with no one wanting it because it was poor soil and lay next to a railroad track. Land that Japanese could afford always lay below dams, near dangerous military sites, swamps, or deserts, or next to railroad tracks—land that no one else wanted. He remembered his father picking up a handful of the dry, sandy soil and letting it sift through his fingers.

"It will take work," his father had said softly. "But it will be ours—in this great new land!"

Seji remembered it all so clearly! Even though his father was not permitted by law to be a citizen, he had loved this country.

Seji remembered going with his father to the bank to borrow the money. Seji had to speak for him because his father spoke only Japanese. Seji had had to learn how to be a business man at a very young age!

He remembered the rejoicing in the family when they were granted the loan and signed the papers. Japanese immigrants could not own property then, but they could put it in a son's name if he had been born in the United States and thus was a citizen.

Seji remembered getting up before dawn to work in the field, helping to reclaim the land. He remembered how his back ached from planting the seedlings, weeding them, watering them, and finally picking the fruit or vegetables.

Each year since the first harvest, things had improved. The ground was good now. Father had found a market where people knew that his produce was good and he could be depended on. He got an excellent price. Life seemed full of promise.

How suddenly things had changed! As Seji stood thinking of these memories, a train went by. He could see that it was crowded with troops. The Japanese had bombed Pearl Harbor on the 7th of December, five months ago. The nation was at war, World War II!

Suddenly all Japanese Americans were not wanted or trusted. All people of Japanese ancestry were believed to be traitors and spies.

Seji had already known about discrimination. When he was in first grade, he couldn't understand English very well. They said he picked on a girl. All he had tried to do was go down the slide first. He may have pushed her, but he hadn't meant to! How can you explain when you are little and people don't understand what you are trying to say?

Now it was much worse. Immediately after the bombing of Pearl Harbor, officials had sent his father to a detention camp many miles inland. Many other Japanese men had been taken away at the same time. Now all Japanese had been ordered to go to Assembly Centers to be sent away. Their leaders were urging them to go quietly. "It is the most patriotic thing you can do for the country," they said.

So the Japanese Americans, not wanting to leave their homes but fearing what might happen if they didn't, were going. Quietly and patiently, they were bearing the unbearable.

A curfew of 8 PM had been imposed on them all. They could go no further than five miles from their homes without a special permit. Wherever they went, there were signs and people saying, "We don't want the Japs here!" or "You can't trust a Jap no matter where he was born!"

Seji had read in the newspaper that the Attorney General of California had said that Japanese farmers "willfully and with malign purpose" had "infiltrated themselves into every strategic spot in our coastal valley counties, such as beside large dams, near airports and miliary training camps, near railroads and power lines."

The injustice of these statements hurt! There had been no proof of any of the things of which they were being accused!

"Why can't people see that we are as good citizens as the Germans and the Italians?" wondered Seji. *They* had not been moved away from *their* homes. They had not been forced to sell their things at a fraction of their value to get cash. The Japanese Americans had had their bank accounts frozen. And now they could take only what they could carry with them. That included bedding and eating utensils.

A few people were standing up for them. They were saying that forcing all the Japanese Americans to leave their homes was unreasonable. It took a lot of courage to say that, because so many people were afraid and hated the Japanese. The United States was losing battle after battle in the war. People were wondering if the Japanese might attack California. Fear filled the air.

Seji looked at the field again. They had been told to plant the crops as usual, even though they were going to be taken away to detention camps. If they didn't, they would be committing sabotage against the United States.

A car was approaching the field, and Seji hurried to greet his old Scout Master, who had agreed to harvest the cantaloupe and go shares on the profit. Seji was anxious to get all the details about the crops arranged. Only a couple of days remained until the family must report to the church where the Japanese-Americans in their area would be picked up.

As they walked around the land, talking about what needed to be done, Seji remembered this man's words when Seji had been a Scout. "There is liberty and justice for all!" he had said. A Scout's honor was very important to this man! Seji had full confidence in him.

"Now I must get home to help my mother pack the things we can't take and must put in storage," said Seji.

Saying good-bye, Seji turned away for the last time from the field that had held so many dreams for the family's future.

In the detention camp in Colorado, Seji sat on the sagging cot in their little room in the barracks. He was opening the box sent by some Caucasian friends from home. Some of their neighbors were remembering them! They had sent some special tea for his mother, books for him, and warm gloves for both of them.

This place was a little better than the Assembly Center they had been taken to at first. That had been a horse's stall at a race track. Just before they had moved into it, the walls had been hastily covered over with tar paper and linoleum had been put on the ground. It reeked of horse!

Here, there was still a barbed wire fence and military guards pacing up and down outside. It was an American concentration camp! They were prisoners without a court hearing, a basic right guaranteed by the Constitution to every citizen of the United States. In their own country, 120,000 Japanese Americans were prisoners of war! Old men, children, women, and even sick people carried into camp on stretchers were considered to be dangerous enemies of the United States!

Seji heard a soft moan from the room next door. The walls were so thin that there was no privacy. Everyone could hear what people next door were saying. Seji knew that the old man next door was not well. It was especially hard for the elderly people to eat strange food and not know if they would live to see their homes again.

The leaders had organized everyone to do the work in the camp. The doctors cared for their health, the nurses worked in the hospital, the teachers taught. Everyone had a job to do. Some of the best educated people were doing the dirtiest jobs in the camp. Gardens were being planted so that people like the man next door would have the fresh vegetables they were used to.

Seji opened another letter that had come that day. It was from the Scout Master. It had bad news! The crop had failed and there was no money coming. Not one cent! How could that be? When he had left, everything had been just right for an excellent harvest!

Seji had heard of people who had had their things lost in unexplained fires. Or the garages had been broken into and their things stolen under very mysterious circumstances! People who had been able to leave their things in the government warehouses seemed to be the lucky ones. Their things were not stolen or burned.

The news in the letter seemed very suspicious. Anger welled up inside Seji. He wanted to strike out and hit someone!

Just then, Seji heard voices outside. He opened the door to see who was there. A man was coming down the path with a guide. He held some packages and a thermos in this hands. He smiled a "hello" to Seji and knocked on the neighbor's door. The elderly man came slowly to open it.

"Herbert Nicholson!" he said in Japanese. "I knew you would come!"

"I brought you a present," Herbert Nicholson answered in Japanese. "I thought that you might like some water from Pasadena."

Tears came to the old man's eyes. Seji felt his eyes sting also. Some people still cared! There were groups who were still trying to correct this terrible injustice. Groups like the American Friends Service Committee were trying to get the Japanese Americans out of the detention camps into communities in the East and Midwest. Seji would gladly work on a farm, harvesting food crops that the nation needed so badly. He wished he could help with the sugar beet crop in Idaho that he had heard was in danger of being lost. He knew what a back-breaking job that was, one that most people didn't want to do!

He turned back into his room. It seemed that just when he was ready to give up and join the angry young Japanese in the camp who wanted to rebel violently, something good happened. Thank God for people who cared!

World War II was over at last, but many memories were burned into Seji's mind. Many were bad ones, such as the dreadful days spent in the camp, losing all the family's property and heirlooms, and the angry and abusive words people said to him on the streets, not only in California but in the East after he had been released from the camp to look for work. There had been threats of violence, a night spent in jail when he had walked down a street in Baltimore, and always angry, suspicious glances as he wandered up and down the eastern coast looking for work.

But there were good memories too, such as the help of many people who got Japanese Americans released from the camps, giving them money to travel by bus to middle and eastern parts of the country. Best of all was the welcome Seji had received when, finally, he had walked into the Friends' meetinghouse on Twelfth Street in Philadelphia. The Friends had found a job for him, working for Bob Warren, a Quaker farmer, in an orchard in New Jersey. Especially wonderful was meeting Emiko and marrying her—and the arrival of their son, Kazuo.

The war was still going on then, and migrant workers were very scarce, but they were badly needed to harvest the important crops. Seji had been able to repay Bob Warren's kindness by telling him of Japanese Americans still in the camps who would be good workers. Bob Warren had sent for them, and some still returned each year to help him at harvest time. Seji was such a good worker that Bob Warren had work for him all year round, even in the winter.

Now they were riding in Bob Warren's car, going to look at an old, dilapidated house on a farm that Bob had bought recently. If it was possible to fix up, Seji and Emiko might have it for a home.

The car crept slowly into the short lane of the falling-down house. In the early spring light, the flat New Jersey landscape faded away across the plowed fields to the distant pine woods.

"It doesn't look like much," Bob Warren apologized. "I'll provide materials and men to help as much as I can. You know how hard it is to get materials even though the war is over."

"We'll do as much as we can ourselves," Seji and Emiko promised. They picked their way around the house through the briars and weeds. Inside, Kazuo enjoyed jumping on the loose floor boards and tapping on the walls.

The next day was a long, hard one for Seji, spent stooping down, picking strawberries. Kazuo tried to help his father and pick with the other men.

"Seji, would you like to go with me in the morning to sell these strawberries" asked Bob, as they loaded the last crate onto the truck. "Kazuo, too."

"Sure!" was Seji's enthusiastic response.

At 5 o'clock the next morning, they were on their way to the big produce center in Philadelphia.

Everything was interesting. Kazuo listened while the men bargained for the load of fruit. But the thing that started Seji thinking was watching Bob Warren sell the strawberries for fifty cents a quart. The day before, he had been paid only five cents a quart for picking them! As he unloaded the truck, he knew that he was in the wrong end of the business. He must find a way to get land and grow crops for sale himself.

The next two months, Seji, Emiko, and Kazuo spent every spare minute fixing up their house. With the help Bob Warren gave them, they were soon able to move into it. The house was fresh, neat, and clean now. The drive was bordered by flower beds bursting with bright colors. The vegetable garden, peeking from behind the house, showed crisp green heads of lettuce, growing in neat rows.

While he had been busy working on the old-new house, Seji had not forgotten his ambition to work for himself. He had been looking around and had found a piece of land that he could rent.

Now was the time to start!

Seji stood before the desk of the vice president in charge of loans in the bank that Bob Warren used. Kazuo, standing quietly beside him, listened while his father asked for a loan.

"You know we can't give you a loan when you have nothing to offer as security," the man was saying, looking down his nose at them. Kazuo felt ashamed and embarrassed. It sounded as though his father should have known that he had no right to ask.

Out in the street they found Bob Warren, who asked if they had found the tool he had sent them to get.

"Yes," Seji answered. He hesitated a moment and then continued. "While we were here, we stopped at the bank to ask for a loan. I have found a piece of land I can rent if I have the money."

"Oh?" Bob paused and then asked, "Did you get the loan?"

"No." Seji's voice sounded discouraged. "I needed something for security."

Bob Warren looked off into the distance for a minute. Kazuo looked at the ground and kicked at a pebble. Was he going to have the same down-the-nose look on his face that the bank man had had?

"Tell you what we'll do," he began. Kazuo looked up quickly. "I hate to lose your help, Seji, but I can understand that you want to start your own business. First thing tomorrow, we'll talk to that man again! I'd be proud to guarantee your loan."

"I'll still work for you," Seji reassured him. "I'll work on my own crop when I'm done with that."

"What are you going to plant?" Bob was curious.

"I thought I would plant early green apple trees," Seji confided.

"That isn't very wise," Bob cautioned. "You never want to plant something that will take so long to mature on rented land. The owner may revoke your lease. Then you will lose the cost of the trees as well as your labor."

At home, Seji wrote the order for the early green apple trees.

"I've just got a feeling about this," he told Emiko, determinedly. "We will have to work hard getting the land ready before the saplings come."

"Won't you need a tractor, just a small one?" Emiko asked.

"We can try," Seji answered. "They are still very scarce. Many farmers need new ones. Waiting lists are very long."

The next day, Seji, with Kazuo tagging along, got out of the old truck in front of a store with a big sign in front that said, "Bailey Brothers Farm Equipment."

Seji didn't see any tractors anywhere. There were a few pieces of rusty second-hand equipment on the lot in back of the building. "We would like to buy a small tractor," Seji told the tall man who came to meet them. Kazuo began to feel scared inside when he saw the expression on the tall man's face. Was he going to look down his nose at them the way the man in the bank had done?

"You know we have a long waiting list," the man was saying to Seji. "Even though the war is over, it takes a long time for a factory to change from making tanks to making tractors. Let me show you the waiting list."

The man pulled out three long papers, covered with names.

"I understand," Seji said softly. "Mr. Warren suggested that I stop and ask you."

"We can put your name on the list," the man said kindly. "But I must tell you that some of our customers have been waiting over three years."

Seji wrote his name at the bottom of the list.

"Didn't I see you at Midville Meeting last Sunday?" the tall man asked as he gathered up the papers.

"Yes, Friends have been kind to us," Seji answered.

It was dark when Seji came into the house a few evenings later. Emiko looked at him anxiously. He looked so tired and thin.

"We'll never get the field ready in time," he said. "The saplings will be here in a few more days."

"A phone call came for you," Emiko handed him a piece of paper. "The man said to call any time before 9 o'clock."

Seji got up slowly and went to the phone. As he gave the operator the number, he looked at Kazuo, whose nodding head was nearly on the table. His son was trying so hard to help! It reminded him of helping his own father with that field beside the railroad tracks. Were they never to get out of this pattern of weary overwork?

Kazuo jerked awake when he heard his father's excited voice. "Mr. Bailey has a small tractor that we can buy!" Seji was telling Emiko as he hung up the phone. It just came in today and we can get it tomorrow!"

"It's like a miracle!" Emiko rejoiced.

"It's the Quakers," Seji replied. "They are really trying to make up for the treatment that the Japanese Americans received during the war."

Because of their hard work and determination, Seji, Emiko, Kazuo, and the brothers and sisters who came later were successful! Starting with an excellent crop of early green apples, their business grew into a very large one.

In a Friends' school there is a beautiful conference room, decorated with lovely Japanese things. It was given to the school by Seji and his family in thanks for the helping hand given to them by many Friends. They have shown their appreciation in many other ways too, but this room stands as a visible reminder to us all that we must speak out courageously against injustice, even when it is unpopular to do so.

LITTLE TREE

By Forrest Carter

Setting: Little Tree was half white, half Cherokee Indian. When he was five years old, his parents died and he went to live with his Cherokee grandparents in the mountains of Tennessee. Here he tells about a day during his first year with them. (Older readers will enjoy the rest of Little Tree's story, too.)

The Way

It had taken Granma, sitting in the rocker that creaked with her slight weight as she worked and hummed, while the pine knots spluttered in the fireplace, a week of evenings to make the boot moccasins. With a hook knife, she had cut the deer leather and made the strips that she wove around the edges. When she had finished, she soaked the moccasins in water and I put them on wet and walked them dry, back and forth across the floor, until they fitted soft and giving, light as air.

This morning I slipped the moccasins on last, after I had jumped into my overalls and buttoned my jacket. It was dark

From *The Education of Little Tree* by Forrest Carter, University of New Mexico Press, 1986. Copyright © 1976 by Forrest Carter. Pp 6-11 reprinted by permission of Eleanor Friede Books, Inc., New York, NY.

and cold — too early even for the morning whisper wind to stir the trees.

Granpa had said I could go with him on the high trail, if I got up, and he had said he would not wake me.

"A man rises of his own will in the morning," he had spoken down to me and he did not smile. But Granpa had made many noises in his rising, bumping the wall of my room and talking uncommonly loud to Granma, and so I had heard, and I was first out, waiting with the hounds in the darkness.

"So ye're up." Granpa sounded surprised.

"Yes, sir," I said, and kept the proud out of my voice.

Granpa pointed his finger at the hounds jumping and prancing around us. "Ye'll stay," he ordered, and they tucked in their tails and whined and begged and ol' Maud set up a howl. But they didn't follow us. They stood, all together in a hopeless little bunch, and watched us leave the clearing.

I had been up the low trail that followed the bank of the spring branch, twisting and turning with the hollow until it broke out into a meadow where Granpa had his barn and kept his mule and cow. But this was the high trail that forked off to the right and took to the side of the mountain, sloping always upward as it traveled along the hollow. I trotted behind Granpa and I could feel the upward slant of the trail.

I could feel something more, as Granma said I would. Mon-o-lah, the earth mother, came to me through my moccasins. I could feel her push and swell here, and sway and give there . . . and the roots that veined her body and the life of the water-blood, deep inside her. She was warm and springy and bounced me on her breast, as Granma said she would.

The cold air steamed my breath in clouds and the spring branch fell far below us. Bare tree branches dripped water from ice prongs that teethed their sides, and as we walked higher there was ice on the trail. Gray light eased the darkness away.

Granpa stopped and pointed by the side of the trail. "There she is—turkey run—see?" I dropped to my hands and knees and saw the tracks: little sticklike impressions coming out from a center hub.

"Now," Granpa said, "we'll fix the trap." And he moved off the trail until he found a stump hole.

We cleaned it out, first the leaves, and then Granpa pulled out his long knife and cut into the spongy ground and we scooped out the dirt, scattering it among the leaves. When the hole was deep, so that I couldn't see over the rim, Granpa pulled me out and we dragged tree branches to cover it and, over these, spread armfuls of leaves. Then, with his long knife, Granpa dug a trail sloping downward into the hole and back toward the turkey run. He took the grains of red Indian corn from his pocket and scattered them down the trail, and threw a handful into the hole.

"Now we will go," he said, and set off again up the high trail. Ice, spewed from the earth like frosting, crackled under our feet. The mountain opposite us moved closer as the hollow far below became a narrow slit, showing the spring branch like the edge of a steel knife, sunk in the bottom. . . .

We sat down in the leaves, off the trail, just as the first sun touched the top of the mountain across the hollow. From his pocket Granpa pulled out a sour biscuit and deer meat for me, and we watched the mountain while we ate.

The sun hit the top like an explosion, sending showers of glitter and sparkle into the air. The sparkling of the icy trees hurt the eyes to look, and it moved down the mountain like a wave as the sun backed the night shadow down and down. A crow scout sent three hard calls through the air, warning we were there.

And now the mountain popped and gave breathing sighs that sent little puffs of steam into the air. She pinged and murmured as the sun released the trees from their death armor of ice.

Granpa watched, same as me, and listened as the sounds grew with the morning wind that set up a low whistle in the trees.

"She's coming alive," he said, soft and low, without taking his eyes from the mountain.

"Yes, sir," I said, "she's coming alive." And I knew right then that me and Granpa had us an understanding that most folks didn't know.

The night shadow backed down and across a little meadow, heavy with grass and shining in the sun bath. Granpa pointed. There was quail fluttering and jumping in the grass, feeding on the seeds. Then he pointed up toward the icy blue sky.

There were no clouds but at first I didn't see the speck that came over the rim. It grew larger. Facing into the sun, so that the shadow did not go before him, the bird sped down the side of the mountain; a skier on the treetops, wings half-folded . . . like a brown bullet . . . faster and faster, toward the quail.

Granpa chuckled. "It's ol' Tal-con, the hawk."

The quail rose in a rush and sped into the trees—but one was slow. The hawk hit. Feathers flew into the air and then the birds were on the ground; the hawk's head rising and falling with the death blows. In a moment he rose with the dead quail clutched in his claws, back up the side of the mountain and over the rim.

I didn't cry, but I know I looked sad, because Granpa said, "Don't feel sad, Little Tree. It is The Way. Tal-con caught the slow and so the slow will raise no children who are also slow. Tal-con lives by The Way. He helps the quail."

Granpa dug a sweet root from the ground with his knife and peeled it so that it dripped with its juicy winter cache of life. He cut it in half and handed me the heavy end.

"It is The Way," he said softly. "Take only what ye need. When ye take the deer, do not take the best. Take the smaller and the slower and then the deer will grow stronger and always give you meat. Pa-koh, the panther, knows and so must ye."

And he laughed. "Only Ti-bi, the bee, stores more than he can use . . . and so he is robbed by the bear, and the 'coon . . . and the Cherokee. It is so with people who store and fat themselves with more than their share. They will have it taken from them. And there will be wars over it . . . and they will make long talks, trying to hold more than their share. They will say a flag stands for their right to do this . . . and men will die because of the words and the flag . . . but they will not change the rules of The Way."

We went back down the trail, and the sun was high over us when we reached the turkey trap. We could hear them before we saw the trap. They were in there, gobbling and making loud whistles of alarm.

"Ain't no closing over the door, Granpa," I said. "Why don't they just lower their heads and come out?"

Granpa stretched full length into the hole and pulled out a big squawking turkey, tied his legs with a thong, and grinned up at me.

"Ol' Tel-qui is like some people. Since he knows everything he won't never look down to see what's around him. Got his head stuck up in the air too high to learn anything.". . .

Granpa laid them out on the ground, legs tied. There were six of them, and now he pointed down at them. "They're al about the same age . . . ye can tell by the thickness of the combs. We only need three so now ye choose, Little Tree."

I walked around them, flopping on the ground. I squatted and studied them, and walked around them again. I had to be careful. I got down on my hands and knees and crawled among them, until I had pulled out the three smallest I could find.

Granpa said nothing. He pulled the thongs from the legs of the others and they took to wing, beating down the side of the mountain. He slung two of the turkeys over his shoulder.

"Can ye carry the other?" he asked.

"Yes, sir," I said, not sure that I had done right. A slow grin broke Granpa's bony face. "If ye was not Little Tree . . . I would call ye Little Hawk."

I followed Granpa down the trail. The turkey was heavy, but it felt good over my shoulder. The sun had tilted toward the farther mountain and drifted through the branches of the trees beside the trail, making burnt gold patterns where we walked. The wind had died in the late afternoon of winter, and I heard Granpa, ahead of me, humming a tune. I would have liked to live that time forever . . . for I knew I had pleased Granpa. I had learned The Way.

NADIA THE WILFUL

By Sue Alexander

In the land of the drifting sands where the Bedouin move their tents to follow the fertile grasses, there lived a girl whose stubbornness and flashing temper caused her to be known throughout the desert as Nadia the Wilful.

Nadia's father, the sheik Tarik, whose kindness and graciousness caused his name to be praised in every tent, did not know what to do with his wilful daughter.

Only Hamed, the eldest of Nadia's six brothers and Tarik's favorite son, could calm Nadia's temper when it flashed. "Oh, angry one," he would say, "shall we see how long you can stay that way?" And he would laugh and tease and pull at her dark hair until she laughed back. Then she would follow Hamed wherever he led.

One day before dawn, Hamed mounted his father's great white stallion and rode to the west to seek new grazing ground for the sheep. Nadia stood with her father at the edge of the oasis and watched him go.

Hamed did not return.

Nadia rode behind her father as he traveled across the desert from oasis to oasis, seeking Hamed.

Nadia the Wilful, Pantheon Books, 1983. Reprinted by permission of Random House, Inc.

Shepherds told them of seeing a great white stallion fleeing before the pillars of wind that stirred the sand. And they said that the horse carried no rider.

Passing merchants, their camels laden with spices and sweets for the bazaar, told of the emptiness of the desert they had crossed.

Tribesmen, strangers, everyone whom Tarik asked, sighed and gazed into the desert, saying, "Such is the will of Allah."

At last, Tarik knew in his heart that his favorite son, Hamed, had been claimed, as other Bedouin before him, by the drifting sands. And he told Nadia what he knew—that Hamed was dead.

Nadia screamed and wept and stamped the sand, crying, "Not even Allah will take Hamed from me!" until her father could bear no more and sternly bade her to silence.

Nadia's grief knew no bounds. She walked blindly through the oasis neither seeing nor hearing those who would console her. And Tarik was silent. For days he sat inside his tent, speaking not at all and barely tasting the meals set before him.

Then, on the seventh day, Tarik came out of his tent. He called all his people to him, and when they were assembled, he spoke. "From this day forward," he said, "let no one utter Hamed's name. Punishment shall be swift for those who would remind me of what I have lost."

Hamed's mother wept at the decree. The people of the clan looked at one another uneasily. All could see the hardness that had settled on the sheik's face and the coldness in his eyes, and so they said nothing. But they obeyed.

Nadia, too, did as her father decreed, though each day held something to remind her of Hamed. As she passed her brothers at play she remembered games Hamed had taught her. As she walked by the women weaving patches for the tents, and heard them talking and laughing, she remembered tales Hamed had told her and how they had made her laugh. And as she watched the shepherds with their flock she remembered the little black lamb Hamed had loved.

Each memory brought Hamed's name to Nadia's lips, but she stilled the sound. And each time that she did so, her unhappiness grew until, finally, she could no longer contain it. She wept and raged at anyone and anything that crossed her path. Soon everyone at the oasis fled at her approach. And she was more lonely than she had ever been before.

One day, as Nadia passed the place where her brothers were playing, she stopped to watch them. They were playing one of the games that Hamed had taught her. But they were playing it wrong.

Without thinking, Nadia called out to them, "That is not the way! Hamed said that first you jump this way and then you jump back!"

Her brothers stopped their game and looked around in fear. Had Tarik heard Nadia say Hamed's name? But the sheik was nowhere to be seen.

"Teach us, Nadia, as our brother taught you," said her smallest brother.

And so she did. Then she told them of other games and how Hamed had taught her to play them. And as she spoke of Hamed she felt an easing of the hurt within her.

So she went on speaking of him.

She went to where the women sat at their loom and spoke of Hamed. She told them tales that Hamed had told her. And she told how he had made her laugh as he was telling them.

At first the women were afraid to listen to the wilful girl and covered their ears, but after a time, they listened and laughed with her.

"Remember your father's promise of punishment!" Nadia's mother warned when she heard Nadia speaking of Hamed. "Cease, I implore you!"

Nadia knew that her mother had reason to be afraid, for Tarik, in his grief and bitterness, had grown quick-tempered and sharp of tongue. But she did not know how to tell her mother that speaking of Hamed eased the pain she felt, and so she said only, "I will speak of my brother! I will!" And she ran away from the sound of her mother's voice.

She went to where the shepherds tended the flock and spoke of Hamed. The shepherds ran from her in fear and hid behind the sheep. But Nadia went on speaking. She told of Hamed's love for the little black lamb and how he had taught it to leap at his whistle. Soon the shepherds left off their hiding and came to listen. Then they told their own stories of Hamed and the little black lamb.

The more Nadia spoke of Hamed, the clearer his face became in her mind. She could see his smile and the light in his eyes, She could hear his voice. And the clearer Hamed's voice and face became, the less Nadia hurt inside and the less her temper flashed. At last, she was filled with peace.

But her mother was still afraid for her wilful daughter. Again and again she sought to quiet Nadia so that Tarik's bitterness would not be turned against her. And again and again Nadia tossed her head and went on speaking of Hamed.

Soon, all who listened could see Hamed's face clearly before them.

One day, the youngest brother came to Nadia's tent calling, "Come, Nadia! See Hamed's black lamb, it has grown so big and strong!"

But it was not Nadia who came out of the tent.

It was Tarik.

On the sheik's face was a look more fierce than that of a desert hawk, and when he spoke, his words were as sharp as a scimitar.

"I have forbidden my son's name to be said. And I promised punishment to whoever disobeyed my command. So it shall be. Before the sun sets and the moon casts its first shadow on the sand, you will be gone from this oasis—never to return."

"No!" cried Nadia, hearing her father's words.

"I have spoken!" roared the sheik. "It shall be done!"

Trembling, the shepherd went to gather his possessions.

And the rest of the clan looked at one another uneasily and muttered among themselves.

In the hours that followed, fear of being banished to the desert made everyone turn away from Nadia as she tried to tell them of Hamed and the things he had done and said.

And the less she was listened to, the less she was able to recall Hamed's face and voice. And the less she recalled, the more her temper raged within her, destroying the peace she had found.

By evening, she could stand it no longer. She went to where her father sat, staring into the desert, and stood before him.

"You will not rob me of my brother Hamed!" she cried, stamping her foot. "I will not let you!"

Tarik looked at her, his eyes colder than the desert night.

But before he could utter a word, Nadia spoke again. "Can you recall Hamed's face? Can you still hear his voice?"

Tarik stared in surprise, and his answer seemed to come unbidden to his lips. "No, I cannot! Day after day I have sat in this spot where I last saw Hamed, trying to remember the look, the sound, the happiness that was my beloved son—but I cannot."

And he wept.

"There is a way, honored father," she said. "Listen."

And she began to speak of Hamed. She told of walks she and Hamed had taken, and of talks they had had. She told how he had taught her games, told her tales and calmed her when she was angry. She told many things that she remembered, some happy and some sad.

And when she was done with the telling, she said gently, "Can you not hear his voice?"

Tarik nodded through his tears, and for the first time since Hamed had been gone, he smiled.

"Now you see," Nadia said, her tone more gentle than the softest of the desert breezes, "there is a way that Hamed can be with us still."

The sheik pondered what Nadia had said. After a long time, he spoke, and the sharpness was gone from his voice.

"Tell my people to come before me, Nadia," he said. "I have something to say to them."

When all were assembled, Tarik said, "From this day forward, let my daughter Nadia be known not as Wilful, but as Wise. And let her name be praised in every tent, for she has given me back my beloved son."

And so it was. The shepherd returned to his flock, kindness and graciousness returned to the oasis, and Nadia's name was praised in every tent. And Hamed lived again—in the hearts of all who remembered him.

NOT SO DIFFERENT AFTER ALL

By Lolly Ockerstrom

Setting: Noriko was a Japanese girl who came to Massachusetts with her mother for several months, where she attended a Quaker school. Here she tells about her first day.

On the first day of school I was nervous. It felt strange not to wear my blue and white uniform. All Japanese students wear uniforms to school. Nobody likes to wear them, but now that I didn't have mine on, I felt uncomfortable, as though I had forgotten something. My mother took me to the Friends School and on the way she told me not to be afraid. "School in USA is different from school in Japan," she said, "but because you go to Friends School in Japan, it will feel a little familiar."

"Quakers in the United States are very kind," she continued. And you'll make new friends and get lots of practice speaking English!"

I did not tell her I did not want to practice English and I did not want to make new friends because I loved my friends in Japan. I did not tell her how scared and homesick I was.

I held my bookbag tightly when the head of the school took me into the classroom. I could see some of my new classmates through the glass window before I went into the room. So many!

And they all had blond hair and big eyes. How would I ever tell them apart? I was introduced to my new teacher, who held out his hand to me. I shook his hand, hoping I was shaking it correctly. "Just call me Tom," he said. This was very strange to me, because in Japan, we never call our teachers by given name. For Tom Sanders we would say "Sanders-sensei." That means "teacher" or "one who knows." It's a special title.

Tom took me into the classroom. "We're working on South Africa," he said. It didn't look like it to me. Some pupils did not even sit at desks, but on the floor. They were in groups, and they were talking to each other. I thought they were rude, but I didn't say so. I wondered why they did not sit straight at their desks and listen to the teacher.

"Class," Tom said, "excuse me for a minute. I'd like to introduce your new classmate. This is Noriko Yamamoto. She is from Tokyo. I'm sure you'll make her feel welcome."

My heart was pounding very fast, and I could feel my face turn red. Everyone was looking at me. I did not know what to do or say, so I bowed. For a moment, no one said anything. Then I heard laughing. A boy in the corner called out, "We don't do that here. You don't have to, either."

I was so ashamed. Of course, I knew that Americans don't bow. But I couldn't help it. I didn't know what to say and I wanted to honor my new classmates. I was embarrassed. I knew I must work hard to remember not to bow. Should I have walked around the room to shake hands with everyone? I wish someone had told me what to do.

I looked up at Tom. He said, "Bowing is a custom in Japan. Perhaps Noriko could tell us about it later. We'll be able to learn a lot about Japanese customs with Noriko here."

Everyone was still looking at me. I tried to speak, but couldn't. I wanted to say something in English, but I was afraid I would make a mistake. I felt my face burning. But my teacher was very kind and showed me my desk. "Perhaps you would like to settle in and get used to your new desk," he said. "You will sit here, next to Andrea." I nodded, although I did not understand what he had said.

I was too nervous to look at Andrea. She leaned over and whispered something I couldn't understand, and touched my arm. Her whisper sounded friendly and her touch was gentle and welcoming. I felt a little better, although I was still too nervous to look at anybody. I pulled out a notebook and put it on the desk. I got a pencil out of my school box and wrote my name in English on the cover. I looked at it. It didn't look like my name. It was only letters from the English alphabet that sounded like my name. I sounded the letters silently to make sure it was really my name. I felt good that I could write my name quickly in English. I wanted to write it in Japanese beneath the English letters, the way I usually do in my English conversation class in Tokyo, but I did not do it. I wanted my notebook to look like everyone else's notebook, and they wrote their names only in English.

I sat up straight and folded my hands on the desk. I did not know where to look because Tom was not at the head of the classroom. I tried to listen, but I could not understand anything! They spoke so quickly! How would I ever learn enough English to be able to speak to them?

I began to think about my school in Tokyo, about my friend Hachiko and my sisters and my father. What were they doing now? I suddenly wanted to cry. What was I doing in this strange city in this strange classroom? I thought about what my calligraphy teacher had said to me before I left Japan: "Wherever you go, God's Light is within you. That Light will never leave you in darkness. You will never be alone. Just trust that you will be led and something good will happen."

But how did she know? She had never been taken to a strange country, where she couldn't even talk to anyone. What good could possibly happen here? I wanted to get up and run out of the classroom, go back to my mother and tell her I wanted to go home to Tokyo today. I didn't want to learn English or make American friends. I wanted to read old Japanese stories and practice making Chinese characters with my calligraphy brush.

Suddenly, I was surprised when all the students stopped talking, and pushed the chairs and desks against the wall. I was very confused. What was happening? Was it an earthquake? I didn't think they had earthquakes in Massachusetts. I started to crawl under my desk. Andrea took my hand and said slowly, "It's time for Quaker Meeting. Will you sit by me?"

I stared at her. I had understood every word she said! She smiled, and I found myself smiling back. I had understood her! And she had understood my confusion. The class gathered into a circle on the floor. I sat next to Andrea, Japanese style with my legs folded under me. In the silence, I could feel a Light shining within me, and I knew I would be OK.

THE CHILDREN
AND THE SALMON

By Marnie Clark

Y uck!" said Karen. "What do you suppose *that* is?" She
pointed to a greenish blob half under water. "Could it be
part of a fender?" She and Nicky couldn't tell. They were
down by Pigeon Creek, near where they lived. So far, that day,
they had seen—in that creek—a toaster, a couple of paint cans,
a diaper, a broken wheelbarrow, and a lot more. It was sicken-
ing.

Karen's mom said that when she was growing up, there
were lots of salmon in Pigeon Creek. Early in the spring, baby
fish would hatch from eggs laid a few months before. The little
fish would swim around in the creek and get bigger. They might
stay a whole year. Then they would start leaving, swimming all
the way down to the mouth of the creek and out into the ocean.
Nobody knew where they went after that, but when they were
four years old, they would somehow find their way back to the
mouth of the very same creek or river and swim up it to the
very same spot where they were hatched, to lay their own eggs.

But that was many years ago. The fish weren't coming any
more now. The water was too polluted. Besides the trash there
were also poisons in the water—soaps and paints and oils and

fertilizers from the new housing developments along the banks. The same thing had happened in the other creeks and rivers.

A few days after their walk by the creek, the children heard that at another creek nearby, a group of neighbors had gotten together and decided to clean up their part of the stream, to make it the kind of place where fish could live. Other groups had heard about it and wanted to do the same thing. Now an official from the County was helping organize a kind of club called "The Adopt-a-Stream Foundation" He was assigning different sections of the rivers to different groups and giving them advice. And the State Department of Fisheries was showing people how to test the water and promising to give them salmon eggs to hatch and put into the water when it was pure enough.

"Would we like to be one of the groups to clean up part of Pigeon Creek and get some fish eggs to hatch?" asked Nicky and Karen's teacher, Brandon King.

"Oh, YES!" the class responded. They could hardly wait to get started. The teacher warned them that it would be a lot of work, and it would be a long time before they would see any salmon come back—at *least* four years. And first of all, they needed to know how to do it right.

So two of the teachers from Jackson School, Vicki Hill and Laurie Baker, took a course at the Foundation and got a grant for supplies. Their section of the creek started a mile from the school. It was about three miles long—a long part to keep track of. It was going to be a project for the whole school.

The first job was to clean it out. Children, teachers, parents, and neighbors all helped. What a mess! Old tires, boxes, bottles, cans, some socks, that old toaster, garbage—all kinds of trash. Three dump trucks were needed to cart it all away! After that, pairs of children checked every week to keep it clean and get water samples to test for poisons.

Meanwhile, other things were happening at the school. Vicki Hill, the first-grade teacher, had a big empty tank to use. The fisheries people brought eggs to put into the tank in January, and about a month later, about 1000 baby fish hatched. The teachers showed the children how to keep the water fresh and cool and later, how to feed the tiny fish. The third- and fourth-graders had the job of feeding them. The fifth-graders kept the tank clean. The little fish stayed in the tank until late spring, growing bigger and stronger.

All the classes were learning about how salmon live and what they need. The children put up signs along the creek that said "DUMP NO WASTE!" They put up posters. They wrote pamphlets and took them to people who lived along the creek. The pamphlets urged people to stop letting fertilizing chemicals get into the creek. They wrote letters to people who were building new housing developments, telling them how important it was to keep pollution out of the creek. Older children wrote articles about their project for the newspapers.

By late May, the tiny fish were over an inch long. They were very thin, but they were strong enough to live outdoors. So one day the children and teachers from one class went down to the creek together with some of the fish. Everybody got to put at least one fish into the water, and they all watched the fish swim around in their big new place. Two classes did that each week until all the baby fish had been put into the creek.

All during the summer and fall and winter, the little fish stayed in that part of the creek. Some died, but most of them grew and got fatter and stronger.

Then, early the next spring, when they were five to six inches long, they started to leave. They swam in the direction the current was going, toward the ocean, miles away. A few days later they were all gone. The creek was empty again. The children wondered if any of them would ever come back. They knew it couldn't be before three whole years. By that time, the original first-graders would be in fifth grade.

All during the next three years, children kept going to the creek each week to keep it clean and get water samples to test. Each winter they got a new load of fish eggs, watched them hatch, fed the baby fish, and released them in the creek in late spring. They kept putting up "DUMP NO WASTE!" signs and taking flyers to the people in the apartments and con-

dominiums and urging the builders to be careful about keeping chemicals and silt out of the stream. They studied stream ecology and learned about soils and what makes a good place for fish to live.

One day, they heard that the Port Authority was planning to build a log storage yard that would nearly block the whole mouth of Pigeon Creek. The children called the newspapers and told them about the plan. When the City Council had a meeting about it, the children and the reporters from the paper were there. The children told the Council members that the mouth of Pigeon Creek should be left open so the salmon could get back upstream to lay their eggs.

Several newspapers printed stories about it, so more people found out about what was happening and started to help. After a while the Port Authority decided to build a smaller storage yard that wouldn't block the mouth of the creek.

Another time, they heard that a group who were watching a different creek had discovered that chlorine had been spilled into the water by mistake at a nearby town. Chlorine is a chemical that can help make drinking water safe, but if it gets into a river, it can kill fish. The government made the town pay a fine and told it to be more careful not to let chlorine get into the river. The government people said they never would have known about the chlorine in the river if it hadn't been for the group that was checking on that part of the river.

So the children knew that what they were doing was important. Sometimes it got pretty tiresome going to check the water, but they kept it up faithfully.

Then one morning, three years after the first young fish had started down toward the ocean, a fifth-grader burst into class in excitement.

"Mr. King! Mr. King! There's a fish in the creek!"

Sure enough, there was! And over the next few days seventeen fish were counted there. Someone had seen a fishing boat at the mouth of their creek, and everyone wondered if some of their other fish had been kept from coming up by being caught.

After the fish started coming back, the children's project got lots of publicity. Their story was written up in several newspapers and magazines, and they were on TV in *Nova* and other programs. Best of all, they discovered that Japanese children were doing the same thing. They sent letters and pictures and artwork to the "Come Back Salmon" group in Tokyo and got letters and pictures back. Later, some of their members even visited each other.

But the effort to bring the salmon back to their normal way of living is not over yet. The second year more fish returned and laid eggs, but some got buried by silt from the runoff from new housing developments and many got washed away because the current was too swift. So none of them hatched that year. It was discouraging.

Sudden gushes of storm water were part of the problem. So the City Council of Everett announced that it would build a big place upstream that would hold the storm water and let it go out it more slowly.

Again hopes were dashed. The plan was cancelled. More discouragement, just as they thought they were winning.

A couple of years later, though, the City Council did build a storage place for storm water—even bigger than the first one they had planned. That kept the current from going too fast after storms.

The third year, about twenty fish came back and laid their eggs. But none hatched. Perhaps the water still needed to be cleaner, or maybe more gravel was needed on the creek bottom.

No one is giving up. By this time, a group of grown-ups called "Stream Keepers" are working for political support. And fish ladders are being put in to help more salmon get up the river at the hardest places. Everybody hopes that next year some of the eggs in the stream will hatch.

Brandon King keeps telling his class, "Always have a dream! Don't let anyone take it away from you. If you get slapped down, get up and try again."

That's just what the children of Jackson School are doing.

PLANTING TREES
TO HEAL THE EARTH

By Janet Sabina and Marnie Clark

Setting: Since Kenya gained its independence in the 1960s, its government has worked hard to modernize the country, but there have been many problems. One is that as more people crowd onto the land, they keep cutting down more trees for space to farm and to get firewood for cooking and heating. Then, without tree roots to hold the dirt together, heavy rains wash the good soil away. New deserts are appearing where forests used to be.

This is the story of how one person is working to make life better for the people of Kenya. She is Wangari Maathai, and her job is not easy.

Wangari Maathai was one of the lucky Kenyan girls to get an education all the way through college. She and other young people in school with her were told they would be future leaders of their country. They would have special responsibility to work to help the Kenyan people. Wangari took this seriously. When she finished school and saw what was happening to the land, she decided to help by planting trees—not a few front yard trees, not even a few hundred trees in a small forest, but thousands of trees, millions even.

Her first project didn't work very well. She was able to get 6,000 free seedlings—tiny trees with small roots and just a few leaves. She decided to get them planted by people who needed work badly. But the people she found to plant them didn't have the tools they needed or enough money for busfare to get to where the work was. And then, because of an especially dry season, the government said no water could be used on gardens. All but two of the little trees died. It was discouraging.

About that time, Wangari went to a United Nations conference in Canada. There she met people like Margaret Mead and Mother Teresa, people with lots of experience working to improve people's lives. She was inspired to keep trying, but she realized she couldn't do it alone.

Wangari went back to Kenya and started a committee of women all over the county. Their first project was to have important leaders plant seven trees in Nairobi, the capital city of Kenya, in honor of seven important Kenyan heroes. They got their pictures in the paper and got a lot of publicity. Unfortunately, the people who were supposed to take care of the trees didn't give them enough water. Before long, they had all died.

Next, Wangari and her committee set a goal of planting millions of trees on public land. People who lived nearby would care for them. They called the project a "Save the Land Harambee." (Ha-rahm-BAY is their word for "Let's all pull together.")

A forestry department of the government liked the women's plans and agreed to give them free seedlings. But when the committee asked for fifteen million seedlings, the forestry people decided they couldn't afford to give away the trees. Fifteen million was just too many.

This gave Wangari another idea. Besides helping the land, she wanted to give power to people who didn't have any. Why not train women to start tree nurseries? Then the women could earn money by supplying the trees she wanted to plant?

This idea worked. Women were shown how to gather seeds from trees that grew naturally in their part of the country. They were taught how to start seedlings and take care of them, and how to run a small business. They were learning to help themselves and help the land at the same time. It was wonderful.

Soon people were planting the right kinds of native trees in long strips to make windbreaks and to hold moisture in the soil. As the seedlings grew and became crowded, they could be thinned. The ones that were taken out could be used for firewood. This was wonderful too.

Radio and TV and newspapers all carried news about the seedlings and young trees. Letters came from schools and churches and public institutions asking for trees to plant. Wangari's idea got a new name. It was called the Green Belt Movement.

People in towns and cities all over Kenya began to form committees. The Green Belt people held meetings to explain how important trees are. They provided garden tools and water tanks and training for the people who were hired to care for the trees. Often they hired people who had handicaps that had made it hard to find work. Hundreds of people found jobs this way.

Wangari discovered that sometimes people planted their seedlings with a lot of enthusiasm and then got tired taking care of them, so many seedlings died. So the Green Belt people tried another new idea. After that, when new trees were planted, they promised to send money to the group for all the trees that were still alive six months after they were planted. Knowing about this money when they started planting made people more anxious to take good care of the little trees while they were getting established in the ground.

Wangari was worried because many tree farmers have been bringing in new kinds of trees to plant because they grow faster and can be cut and sold sooner than trees that grow naturally in Kenya. People have found that they can make money quickly this way. But trees that are only planted to be cut down in a few years don't solve the problem of soil being washed away. Equally important, these trees upset the natural balance of nature. Besides firewood and building material, the native trees of Kenya also provide animal fodder, fruits, honey, and herbal medicines, that the imported trees do not.

Wangari is working hard to teach people that the native trees are better for Kenya. And she can see that her efforts have made a difference. In only twelve years, 15 hundred community tree nurseries have been started. Over 10 million native trees have been planted on public lands by the Green Belt Movement. Many of them are in green belts near schools and are taken care of by schoolchildren. Over a million children do this work. Each child takes care of one or two trees.

In 1989 Wangari Maathai was given $10,000 by Global Windstar Awards for her tree-planting and environmental work in Kenya. People wondered what she would do with all that money. At the award ceremony she announced that she would give it to young tree nurseries and green belt committees in other parts of Africa.

Wangari Maathai is not a Quaker, but she talks about "that of God" in us all. She believes "that of God" is our ability to care about people—all people—and about our precious earth.

THE CHILDREN'S ETERNAL RAIN FOREST

By Ilse O. Reich

I n a small town in Sweden a few years ago, an elementary school teacher, Mrs. Kern, was teaching her class about the tropical rain forests in Central and South America. She told them about the colorful birds that live there, from tiny hummingbirds to the very rare Quetzal with its long red tail, about the rare insects and plants, the snakes and frogs and monkeys and even some jaguars and other wild animals. She told them about the unusual flowers that grow there and how some trees grow very tall to catch the sun above the clouds that often hang over the damp forests. Sometimes the forests are so high in the mountains that they have clouds around them much of the time and are called cloud forests.

Mrs. Kern told them that these special forests were in great danger because in many places they were being cut down or burned to get open space. She told them that in Costa Rica the Quakers in the Monteverde community have set aside a rain forest preserve where no one is allowed to cut down the trees or hunt the animals or damage the rare plants.

Suddenly one of the boys in her class asked, "Mrs. Kern, what can we do to help save the rain forests?" The boy's name was Roland, and he was nine years old.

Mrs. Kern didn't know what to say. "What do *you* think you could do?" she asked the children. They talked excitedly for a while, and several children had ideas. The idea everyone liked best was to think of ways to earn money and then use the money to buy more acres to add to the Cloud Forest Reserve in Monteverde.

Roland and the other children went right to work. They baked cookies with ingredients that grow in the rain forest, like vanilla, chocolate, and ginger. They made paintings of the flowers and animals of the rain forest. They made Christmas cards to sell. They wrote poems, songs, and plays about the need to save the forests, the plants, and the animals. They asked their parents and grandparents to buy an acre of rain forest in their name as a birthday or Christmas present.

People in other towns heard about what they were doing and invited them to their schools to sing their songs and perform their plays, and that got *those* children interested in saving the rainforests.

That year, 1987, Roland and his class collected enough money to buy fifteen acres of cloud forest. It was used to start a special protected area called the Children's Eternal Rain Forest.

The Swedish government was proud of the children and contributed money to buy more acres. Pretty soon the Costa Rican Ambassador in Sweden heard about what the children had done and went to visit Roland's school. The result was that the government of Costa Rica invited Roland, nine of his classmates, and their teacher and her husband to visit Monteverde and see the forest that their money had saved.

The Quaker Community in Monteverde had a supper for them at the meetinghouse, and the children of the Monteverde Friends School, their parents, and their Costa Rican neighbors were all invited. The Swedish children sang some of their songs and performed some of their dances and plays and invited the Montverde children to take part. Soon all the children were singing and dancing together. Although they couldn't speak each others' languages, they didn't seem to have much trouble understanding each other.

After that, Roland and his group spent three days hiking on the muddy trails of the rain forest. Then they washed away the mud and went to San José, where the President of Costa Rica had a good-bye party for them.

And even that was not all. Soon after they returned to Sweden, the King of Sweden decided to visit their school. The King and Queen both came, and of course they were greeted by the children waving flags. The King and Queen shook hands with the teachers, and the children sang their rain forest songs. The King was very touched and impressed with what these children had accomplished.

Even *that* is not the end of the story. Children in other countries heard about how the Swedish children had raised money to buy acres of rain forest. They wanted to help too. So now other children in the United States, Canada, England, Japan, and of course Sweden and Norway are busy collecting money to save more acres.[1]

In 1991, as this is written, the "Bosque Eterno de los Ninos" (the Childrens Eternal Rain Forest) has over 18,000 acres in it, and the effort of children, parents, and teachers all over the world continues.

---

[1] The address to write to in the United States is: The Children's Rain Forest, P.O. Box 936, Lewiston, Maine 04240.

WHO OWNS THE SEA?

By Marnie Clark

In 1967, ocean explorers discovered lots of funny-looking little lumps that looked like burned baked potatoes on the bottom of the Pacific Ocean out near Hawaii. Though they didn't look like much and were three miles down, they had manganese and nickel and other valuable metals in them. Some of those metals were getting scarce in our mines, so people were excited about the idea of getting metals from the seabed. One company started to make a machine like a huge vacuum cleaner to suck up the lumps.

At the United Nations, a delegate named Arvid Pardo, from the tiny country of Malta, had an idea. He thought that the wealth of the ocean bottom, out beyond the parts near coastlines, should belong to everybody, not just to the countries rich enough to take it.

"There are already fights about the fish and warnings that too many are being caught," said Pardo. "Soon there may be fights about these metal lumps on the bottom of the sea. How much better for us to decide that this wealth belongs to all of us! Let's work together to make a law to say how the oceans will be used so that everyone will benefit, even the poorest countries."

It was an exciting new idea. This could make the world a more fair place, and prevent a lot of fights too.

So the United Nations began to plan a special conference to make a law for the sea. They would talk about fishing rights and the rights of ships to go near other nation's coastlines, and how far out the countries with coastlines could claim, and what rights countries without any coastline should have, and who could sail where without being stopped, and where ships would need permission to go. They would talk about who would have a right to go after those manganese lumps on the bottom of the sea, and how the profits would be used.

By that time, there was something else they needed to talk about too: pollution! Radioactive waste and toxic chemicals were being dumped in the oceans. Oil tankers were flushing out their tanks at sea, and sometimes there were bad oil spills. Many harbors were badly polluted. The good fishing grounds near the coastlines were getting polluted from industries, and the poisons were hurting the fish. All the countries would need to work together to protect the oceans from pollution!

Naturally, planning such a big conference took a long time. A year passed, and another. And another. The conference was to begin in 1973, and there was still a lot to do.

Then, in 1972, two Quakers in the Blue Ridge Mountains of Virginia made an important decision. One evening, after inspecting his orchard, Sam Levering, explained to his wife Miriam what he had been mulling over in his mind.

"You know, Miriam, you and I have been working for peace in a number of ways through the years. When someone asks what I do, I often say, '50 percent apples and 50 percent world peace.' Now, with this year's apple crop damaged by frost, I will have more time for peace. Let's serve full time for a while with the Friends Committee on National Legislation in Washington." They knew that two Philadelphia Quakers, William Fischer and Barton Lewis, had already asked the Committee to work on the Law of the Sea Conference.

Miriam was enthusiastic. "I'm with you, Sam!" she said. "World peace needs all the help it can get."

Little did the Leverings know that they would be spending a major part of their time for the next ten years helping make the Law of the Sea become a reality. Their first challenge came when Sam found that the United States Congress had been asked to say OK to mining companies who wanted to start scooping up those lumps from the bottom of the sea. The companies were anxious to get started before the new sea law could control what they did.

Right away, Sam and Miriam called the Quaker United Nations Office in New York to get help reaching the people who were planning the Law of the Sea Conference. Soon Sam had a meeting with them to explain why it was important to get the Conference started as soon as possible. He helped the planning get finished and helped the U.S. protect the Conference by not letting the mining companies start mining those valuable lumps.

The first session of the Conference was in 1973 in New York. The delegates made two important decisions. First, they would tackle all the problems about the oceans that needed a world law—not just fishing and shipping and mining, but also protecting the seas and the creatures that live in them. Second, they decided that they would keep having meetings until they had a treaty ready for all the nations to sign. It was lucky they decided that, because they never could have finished quickly.

Problems started right away. The countries that didn't have coastlines wanted their share of the sea's riches. But how much was their share? How far out from shore should a country have control? Should private companies do mining on the ocean floor, or should some new United Nations agency do it? Which waters should be free for anyone to sail through, and did that mean warships or just trading ships? How could the sea environment be kept clean enough for fish to live in? What should happen if someone broke the rules? People got pretty excited defending their own points of view.

Sam and Miriam found several ways to help. One way was to invite delegates from different parts of the world to small meetings where they could hear experts talk about one of the problems and some of the ways it might be solved. Then the delegates could discuss it and hear each others' ideas and gradually begin to see what would be best for all. They learned more by listening, and they became more patient with each other because they understood better how things looked to people from other parts of the world.

Another way Sam and Miriam helped was by putting out a newspaper, *Neptune*, named for the Roman God of the sea. It was written for all the delegates to the Conference. In it they shared what they had learned from the experts and from the discussions in their small meetings. They also told where progress was being made. They gave copies to all the delegates at the Conference.

By this time, the delegates were all working in small groups on particular parts of the new law. That made it hard for them to know what was happening in other groups. The *Neptune* newspaper helped them keep up-to-date on the whole thing. It told where problems had been solved and helped them keep their excitement about this big new idea that they were working on. It helped them not get discouraged.

By this time Sam and Miriam had attracted a team of volunteers, mostly young people, to work with them. Some helped produce *Neptune;* others collected information or talked to groups about the Conference and the need for a sea law. One took his sailboat to towns along the coast, where he made speeches about saving the sea life.

Sam and Miriam helped in another way. Sometimes delegates would have ideas they wanted to present to their group or to a larger part of the Conference. Sam would help them get their papers ready, making them as clear as possible. Sometimes he would suggest new ideas that the delegates would like so much they wanted to include them.

Over the next ten years, there were many meetings in different parts of the world. It took hard work and a lot of patience. But finally a Law of the Sea treaty was ready for the nations to sign. One part had rules about all the long-time questions about boundaries, fishing rights, shipping, and so on. A second big part was about protecting the sea environment and doing scientific research. A third part was about the seabed—the bottom of the ocean out beyond the control of any country where the manganese lumps were. A new International Seabed Authority would be in charge of that. The details of just how it would work would be finished after the treaty as a whole was signed. The new law also had a big section on how disagreements would be taken care of. A new court would be set up to deal with violations of the law or settle arguments that could not be worked out peacefully by the countries themselves.

In 1982 the delegates met in Jamaica to sign the new treaty. More than 140 did sign it, and the Preparatory Commission started its work of planning the court and other new agencies that the law said there should be.

Since then, as this is being written, the governments of 47 nations have ratified the treaty. That means they have agreed to follow it. When 60 countries ratify it, it will become *Treaty Law* for those countries. Treaty Law can be enforced by courts.

The United States had been helping all during the ten years of meetings, but a sad thing happened in Jamaica. The new Reagan administration in Washington said it wouldn't sign the treaty with so many details still to be worked out, and it wouldn't even take part in the Conference work any more. A little later, it did say that it would accept most of the new law as *Customary International Law* and follow its rules. But until the United States signs and ratifies the new law, it can't be *made* to follow the Law of the Sea if it decides it doesn't want to.

If it hadn't been for those funny-looking lumps, the Law of the Sea would have been finished long ago. Many people hope that the final details can be worked out so all the main countries will ratify it. Then it will become law that can be enforced. If that happens, the international seabed will at last become the common heritage of all the people of the world.

THE MONTEVERDE COMMUNITY

By Marnie Clark

T he Quakers in Fairhope Meeting, Alabama, were excited when the United States helped start the United Nations in 1945. There had just been four hard years of war in Europe and in the Pacific, and near the end the United States had dropped atomic bombs on two Japanese cities. Surely now, they thought, there would never be another war. With atom bombs, war would be too horrible, and with the new UN to help, countries would be able to solve their arguments in peaceful ways, without fighting.

But it didn't work out that way. The soldiers came home, but the United States kept building more weapons, and the taxes to pay for them kept going up. People were warned that this was necessary because the Russians were dangerous and wanted to fight the United States.

In fact, just in case a war might start, a law was passed that said all young men between 18 and 26 must sign up to be ready to go into the army. It was the first time this had ever happened here during peacetime. One reason many immigrants had come to the United States in the past was to get away from being forced into the army.

In the Fairhope Meeting was a young many named Wilford Guindon. Everybody called him "Wolf." He had just turned eighteen. Two others in the Meeting—Howard and Leonard Rockwell—were over eighteen too. All three of these young men said they would never be able to kill anyone, even if the government told them to. They believed it was wrong for the government to force young men to go into the army to fight and kill. So they refused to cooperate with the army at all and didn't even go to the office to give their names.

The Rockwell boys' Uncle Marvin did the same thing. He had been a medic in the army in the European war, but he wasn't 26 yet, so he was supposed to sign up and maybe go to war again. He had come to believe that he just shouldn't cooperate with the military system at all, even to register his name.

The four young men knew they were breaking the law, but they felt they were following a higher law, God's law, that says people should care about and help each other, not kill them.

Of course, the government didn't let them get away with that. They were all arrested and tried in a court in Mobile. When Wolf and the others explained why they would not have anything to do with the army system, the judge listened carefully. He seemed sympathetic, but clearly they were disobeying the law, so he sentenced them all to prison in Florida. Then he said, "If you don't like this country's laws, you should go to another country."

Even before the judge said that, the members of Fairhope Meeting had talked about the possibility of finding a country where their children wouldn't have to choose between killing people and going to prison. Could they maybe even find a place where there weren't commercials on radio and ads everywhere urging people to buy fancy things they didn't need? Several people wanted a simpler life style where people and contact with nature were more important than things.

Several of the people in the Fairhope Meeting were farmers. They were interested in other ways of farming and curious about how farmers in other places did things. Two members,

Hubert and Mildred Mendenhall, went on a farm tour to see farming in Central American countries. One of the places they visited was the tiny country of Costa Rica. While they were there, they met the government person in charge of agriculture. They learned that the government of Costa Rica was doing many things to help ordinary people have a better life. And there was no army! The Costa Rican government had decided it was better to use its money for things the people needed, like learning to read and being able to own land.

When the Mendenhalls got back home with this news, many families began to talk seriously about moving to Costa Rica. It was a big decision. Did they really want to leave their jobs and comfortable homes and store-bought conveniences and go far away from all their relatives and friends who thought life in the United States was OK? Could they earn a living in Costa Rica? What would life there be like, with all their neighbors speaking Spanish? Could they give their children a good education? It would be a big change!

The more they talked about it, the more sure several families became that they wanted to go. The ones who were already farmers thought it wouldn't be too big a change to be farmers somewhere else. Most of their children were already going to a small school that the Meeting was running. The teacher, Mary Mendenhall, wanted to go, so they could just take the school along! Wouldn't it be wonderful to build a whole new community where everyone would be free to carry out Jesus' teachings of love and nonviolence, where everyone would work for the good of everyone else!

The young children were excited about it, ready for the new adventure. It was harder for the older children, who realized what a big change it would be and were afraid they would miss high school in the United States, plus the sports and social life they were beginning to enjoy.

About half the families in the Meeting decided to go together as soon as the young men's prison terms were over. They were pleased when they received encouragement from the Costa Rican Consul in New Orleans and even a letter of welcome from the President of Costa Rica. Many reporters came to interview them. It was pretty unusual for a whole group of families to be leaving the United States to make a community somewhere else. Some of the reporters were critical; others were sympathetic. Some wished they could go too.

In November 1950 the first families left for Costa Rica. Others followed as soon as they could sell their property and make arrangements. A few months later, nine families were in San Jose, the capital city of Costa Rica. The youngest person was 1, the oldest one 80. Wolf and his new bride "Lucky" were among them, and another newly married couple too. There were families with children, two sets of grandparents, and a few young men who didn't have families yet.

In the city of San José, they rented places to live and also a house on a coffee farm. Here they set up their school in a coffee shed. Some of the men used two jeeps to explore the countryside looking for good land. It took five months, but they finally found just the right place—land high on the mountain-side between the two seas. The mists from the Atlantic Ocean kept the fields green and good for farming, and it was high enough to be cool and comfortable even in summer. They named it *Monteverde*, meaning "green mountain."

The only trouble was that there was no road to it for the last twelve miles. So their first job was to build a road good enough for the jeeps to go up. After that, it took a couple of months to take all the people and their belongings up the mountain in the two jeeps. Even after the road was finished, they would often have to stop on their way up or down to clear away a mudslide or a fallen tree before they could go on.

The first thing they did was to divide their land into two parts. The lower part could be cleared and used for farming. In fact, some of the land had already been cleared and there were a few Costa Rican farmers not far away. After a lot of discussion and some persuasion by one couple, who were biologists, they agreed that the beautiful tropical rain forest on the higher part of their land would be set aside and protected. In it was the source of the Guacimal River, which provided water and power to all who lived near it, all the way down to the ocean. A great many people could enjoy the beauty of the forest, and scientists could study the rare birds, animals, and plants there. They called it a cloud forest because often its mountain tops were in clouds formed by mists on the Atlantic Ocean side, where it rained a lot. Often they saw beautiful double rainbows, sometimes even triple ones.

On the property they found a small saw mill and a house that had belonged to the owner. Many stayed in that house at first, while tents were being put up. School was held there, too, as well as Meeting for Worship twice a week and a town meeting, which met often to make plans and work out problems together. For a long time there was no electricity, and they had to carry water from the river or springs.

To build houses, they had to make boards first! So they cleared land for space for houses and farms, and then they used the saw mill to make boards out of the trees they had cut down. Then they were ready to start building.

From the beginning, they had lots of "bees." These were times when they worked together to build someone's house or repair the roads or cooperate on some other job. Many of their houses were built that way, and as time went on, they had bees for building and repairing the school and meetinghouse, for building a library and a carpenter shop, and for many other projects.

With no electricity or gas, they had to cook on wood-burning stoves and learn what woods were best for burning. They churned their own butter and made bread. With no nearby stores, they grew their own food and made most of what they needed, including clothes for themselves and their chidlren. They even made jeans and denim jackets.

Some of the women learned to be midwives, so they could help each other when babies were born. The first baby was born in a tent. Meanwhile, visitors came, and some of the visitors decided to stay.

The children soon found that horses were better than bicycles for getting around in the hilly country. Children learned to milk cows, feed chickens, gather eggs, bring in wood for the kitchen stove, harvest corn, bring in bananas, and help at house-building bees. The grownups said they couldn't have done it all without the children's help.

The land was better for animals than for crops because it was so hilly. One family had goats for a while; some raised pigs. Some Costa Rican dairymen helped them start good dairy herds by selling good young heifers and lending them a fine bull.

Soon they realized that they would have more milk than they could use, but how could they sell it? There was no way they could take big cans of fresh milk down that rough road to the city, and during the rainy season each year there was a long time when they couldn't use the road at all. They needed something to sell that wouldn't take much space and wouldn't spoil in bad weather. Why not use the extra milk to make cheese?

Several families decided to start a cheese factory together, and there was a bee to build the first building for it. They agreed that only people who lived there could own shares in the factory so all the money they earned selling the cheese would stay there in the community. At first, they agreed to wait for payment for their milk until the cheese was sold so all the factory's money could be used for making cheese.

It was three years after the first families had arrived at Monteverde when the factory started making cheese. Young boys delivered the milk on horseback early in the morning. The first cheese was pressed in Quaker Oats cans, but later it was made in big round molds.

When a load was ready, a four-wheel-drive truck would take it down to the city to sell. The truck would return several days later with supplies for the families. The trip down to the city took all day, and sometimes the truck would break down. One time the whole back of the truck fell off, and the cheese fell out. The truck had to be welded together and reloaded with the cheese before it could continue down the mountain.

Before long, many Costa Rican neighbors were selling milk to the cheese factory too. That meant building a bigger building and hiring more workers. Community members took turns working on Sundays and holidays so it could keep running every day. When repairs were needed, they were made at night. By this time, they had a rebuilt generator to make electricity, using water power from the river that ran through their land.

The school grew too. Ten years after their arrival at Monteverde, the school had 23 pupils. Eight were Costa Rican children, so it was important for everyone to be able to speak both English and Spanish. Five young people had graduated from high school and had no trouble getting into good colleges in the United States. Mary Mendenhall was still the Head Teacher.

Teachers came from Holland and Spain as well as the United States; one teacher had spent many years in Japan. Besides the regular teachers, there were many people in the community with special skills and knowledge to share. Sometimes the scientists who came to study the cloud forest would teach the children. Several times teachers from the United States came down to teach special courses. Grades 1 through 12 were taught as there were children needing them. Older children helped younger ones. They seldom had homework because they all had so much to do to help at home. Every four years, everyone who was in high school got to go on a five-day trip to visit interesting places around Costa Rica, like the University, industries, volcanoes, theater programs, and the National Assembly.

Before the last day of school, the teachers and children would work to get the building and yard all clean and in good shape, and after the work they would have a big bonfire and picnic. At the "Last Day of School Program," the whole school had plays, choral readings, and singing in both Spanish and English, and the children gave each teacher a gift that they had made. When a senior class graduated, there was a banquet the evening before, put on by the junior class, with place cards, decorations, and a class prophecy. On graduation day there would be a special speaker, speeches written and read by the seniors, and diplomas for the graduates.

On Christmas Eve the children and young people went caroling to every house in the community and to some of the Costa Rican neighbors. Names had been drawn for gifts, so each person gave—and received—one gift. All were home made. On Christmas Day, after Meeting for Worship there was a Community Christmas dinner, and after dinner the gifts were passed out by some of the small children from a beautifully decorated tree. Such a variety! Leather work, shirts, dolls, toys, embroidered pillow cases, and on and on. Then there was more carol singing before everyone went home.

Over the years there have been many changes. A cooperative women's craft group was started. A restaurant was opened and one family started to prepare and sell snacks for scientists and tourists. The Monteverde Conservation League was formed to work on protection of the cloud forest and educate people about the environment. There is a Monteverde Institute, an educational group that fosters cultural and scientific activities and arranges opportunities for university courses for students and teachers from colleges and universities in the United States. It also helps plan musical and theatrical opportunities in the Monteverde community. Many tourists as well as scientists visit the cloud forest each year.

In 1988, the big rains from a hurricane brought a wall of mud and trees down the hill and pushed Wolf and Lucky's house off its foundation. The family moved into rooms above the barn, and a couple of months later the whole community turned out to shovel away the dirt and begin to raise the house for a new foundation.

Not all the new families who have come are Quakers. But those who stay agree that happiness comes not from material possessions but from living a meaningful life. The members of the Monteverde community feel they are very much a part of the world community, sharing common concerns for peace, social justice, and a livable planet.

=====

The Friends General Conference Religious Education Committee seeks to act as a catalyst for Quaker spiritual development at the monthly, quarterly, and yearly meeting levels, as well as within individual Friends. We provide workshops, retreats, and curriculum materials, and work through other FGC programs such as the Gathering and the Quarterly. Religious education programs have been central to the mission of FGC since its founding almost 100 years ago.

=====

Friends General Conference is an association of yearly meetings and monthly meetings which exists to nurture the life of the Spirit in Friends' personal lives, in corporate worship, in the meeting community, and in the world. Its work is accomplished by hundreds of volunteers from every affiliated meeting and a staff headquartered in Philadelphia.

=====